MASSACRE!

Below in the camp lay the bodies of three hideously slaughtered white men. Slowly, Touch the Sky became aware of all the whiskey bottles scattered throughout the camp. Spotting more unopened bottles in cases lashed to the mules, the youth realized what had probably happened. The murderers had made their victims stuporous with strong water, then killed them in their sleep.

The scene was so horrible that Touch the Sky nearly cried out when a hand fell on his shoulder. But it was only Little Horse, showing him that Back Elk was signaling the retreat.

"We must return to camp at once and report this in council!" Black Elk said. "I care nothing if the paleface devils slaughter one another. But I fear a great storm of trouble will soon come—these killings were done so as to seem that red men did them!"

The *Cheyenne* Series:

#1: ARROW KEEPER

CHEYENNE

2

DEATH CHANT
JUDD COLE

LEISURE BOOKS **NEW YORK CITY**

A LEISURE BOOK®

November 1992

Published by

Dorchester Publishing Co., Inc.
276 Fifth Avenue
New York, NY 10001

Printed in the United States of America.

Prologue

In 1840, when the new grass was well up, Running Antelope and 30 braves rode out from their camp on the Powder River. The great Northern Cheyenne chief was troubled by the vast number of Bluecoats and gold-hungry whites swarming into the best hunting grounds of the sacred Cheyenne homeland.

Running Antelope was not leading his braves into battle, but to an important council with their kinsmen the Southern Cheyenne, who lived below the Platte River. His wife Lotus Petal and their infant son accompanied him in order to visit her southern clan.

Running Antelope's band flew a white truce flag. Nonetheless, a company of Bluecoat pony soldiers ambushed them in a surprise pincers movement near the North Platte. Badly outnumbered, the Cheyenne with their bows, lances, clubs and single-shot muzzle-loaders were no match for the Bluecoats' big-thundering wagon guns and percussion-cap carbines. Soon Running Antelope, Lotus Petal, and all 30 braves lay dead or dying. The lone survivor was the squalling infant.

His life spared by the Bluecoat lieutenant in charge, the baby was taken back to the riverbend settlement of Bighorn Falls near Fort Bates. The barren wife of John Hanchon, owner of the town's mercantile store, fell in love with the young orphan and insisted on raising him as their own son.

The Hanchons named him Matthew. He grew into a tall, broad-shouldered youth with the pronounced cheekbones and even, pleasing features that had earned the Cheyenne the name of the Beautiful People among their red brothers. Matthew's parents were good to him, and despite occasional hostile glances and remarks from some white men, he felt accepted in his limited world.

Then came his sixteenth year and a forbidden love for Kristen, the daughter of Hiram Steele, the wealthiest rancher in Bighorn Falls. Discovered in their secret meeting place, Matthew was savagely beaten by Steele's hired hand Boone Wilson, then driven off Steele's property under threat of death if he returned. Then a young officer from Fort Bates, eager to win Kristen's hand in marriage, threatened to ruin John Hanchon's profitable contract with the fort if Matthew did not clear out for good.

Saddened, but determined to find a place where he fit in, the youth left his home and white parents forever. He rode north into the hostile Cheyenne country of the Southeastern Montana Territory. Matthew was soon captured by Cheyenne braves. His white man's language, customs, and clothing made the Indians suspect he was a spy for their enemies.

He was brutally tortured. Only the intervention of old Arrow Keeper, the tribal medicine man, spared him from death at the point of a knife. Arrow Keeper had recently experienced a powerful vision at sacred Medicine Lake. The vision prophesied the arrival of the son of a great chief who would eventually lead his people in victorious battle against their enemies. The new leader would bear the mark of a warrior—a mulberry-colored arrowhead. When Arrow Keeper found that birthmark buried past the captured youth's hairline, he knew the vision had been fulfilled. But, fearing that this knowledge might cause great trouble in the tribe, Arrow Keeper kept it to himself, choosing to reveal the truth of his vision only after the newcomer had proven himself.

At Arrow Keeper's urging, the suspected spy's life was spared and he was allowed to join the tribe's young males, who were training to become warriors. Renamed Touch the Sky by Arrow Keeper, the youth at first had only one ally besides the old medicine man: Honey Eater, the beautiful young daughter of Chief Yellow Bear. The rest of the tribe hated him, especially a warrior named Black Elk and his bitter young cousin, a warrior-in-training called Wolf Who Hunts Smiling.

A surprise Pawnee attack destroyed the Cheyenne village and killed many warriors. Black Elk, whose love for Honey Eater made him resent her secret glances at Touch the Sky, was ordered to quickly train the younger males for battle. The tribe was determined to achieve revenge against their Pawnee attackers.

From the beginning Touch the Sky was tormented and humiliated. He could do nothing right: he could not ride bareback, throw a spiked tomahawk, hunt buffalo, or even sharpen a knife Indian fashion. Despite those failures, his courage and determination to succeed eventually won the

7

friendship of a warrior-in-training named Little Horse. But Wolf Who Hunts Smiling had vowed to kill Touch the Sky, and he was always watching for an opportunity to make good on his oath.

Soon a huge band of Pawnee warriors again encircled the village, preparing to annihilate the badly outnumbered Cheyenne. Touch the Sky, knowing the lopsided battle would surely destroy the tribe, remembered something important from his life among the white men: a Bluecoat soldier had once explained to him that the Pawnee believed that insane white people were powerful bad medicine.

Through great skill, cunning, and bravery, he and Little Horse applied their recent training and infiltrated the Pawnee lines. They raced desperately toward Bighorn Falls and the home of Touch the Sky's boyhood friend Corey Robinson. After Corey agreed to help save the tribe, Touch the Sky and the others hurried back to the camp, praying they would not arrive too late.

Dawn broke over the Tongue River and the Pawnee attack began. But Corey Robinson, his naked white body streaked with redbank clay, suddenly appeared, capering like a lunatic and loudly spouting gospel. Shrieking in fear, the Pawnee showed the white feather and fled.

Touch the Sky had saved his tribe and was honored in a special council. But as Arrow Keeper cautioned him, it was white man's cunning he displayed, not the true Cheyenne way. And now more than ever Black Elk and Wolf Who Hunts Smiling hated Touch the Sky.

Though elated when Honey Eater secretly declared her love, the youth was neither a full warrior nor accepted by the tribe. Touch the Sky was also sobered by Arrow Keeper's warning that there would be many trials and much suffering before he ever raised high the lance of leadership.

Chapter 1

"Hiya, hi-i-i-ya!"

Screaming the shrill war cry of his tribe, the tall, broad-shouldered Cheyenne youth dug his heels into the flanks of his spirited dun pony. His left arm gripped the pony's neck. His right was raised high over his head, a double-bladed throwing ax clutched tight in his fist.

Dressed in beaded leggings, a breechclout, and elkskin moccasins, he had a strong, hawk nose, and his mouth was set in a straight, determined slit. His hair hung in long, loose locks, except where it was cropped close over his brow to keep his vision clear. The locks streamed almost straight out behind him as the pony reached a full gallop.

"Hiya, hi-i-i-ya!"

As he came abreast of a huge cottonwood he released the ax. It twirled end over end and then sliced into the

9

tree with a solid *thuck*. A smaller youth, standing among a group of five Cheyenne watching from a nearby hummock, ran toward the tree to retrieve the ax. It was necessary to brace one foot against the cottonwood before he managed to pry the deeply embedded weapon loose.

Touch the Sky slowed his dun to a trot and turned her back in the direction of the others. When he rode up, the oldest Cheyenne stepped forward. Called Black Elk, he had seen 20 winters. He was the only full warrior in the group.

"At least now no blood flows from your pony," Black Elk said.

The warrior held his face impassive in the Indian way. His fierce appearance was made even fiercer by the leathery chunk of his right ear, which had been severed in battle and crudely sewn back on with buckskin thread.

Touch the Sky felt warm blood creeping up the back of his neck. But he said nothing. Black Elk's remark was a mocking reference to his first attempt to throw an ax from horseback, several moons earlier when Black Elk had first begun training the youths. Then the ax had ricocheted off the wrong tree and wounded his own pony.

Despite his shame, Touch the Sky, too, held his face impassive. Vividly, he recalled the time when he had first joined Yellow Bear's tribe and his white man's habit of letting his emotions show in his face had earned him the insulting name Woman Face.

Little Horse, who had retrieved the ax, spoke up in admiration of his friend's skill. "Had this been a lice-eating Pawnee instead of a tree, he would be in two bloody pieces!"

Black Elk took the ax from Little Horse, saying nothing. But a youth named Wolf Who Hunts Smiling spoke up scornfully. "This is nothing! Even a blind squirrel will root up an acorn now and then!"

Wolf Who Hunts Smiling, who belonged to the Panther clan, was Black Elk's younger cousin. He was bigger and older than all the others, with the exception of Touch the Sky. He had a wily face befitting his name, with furtive eyes that followed every move of whomever he watched. Now those eyes were filled with hatred for Touch the Sky. Wolf Who Hunts Smiling had seen his father cut down by Bluecoat canister shot, and he fiercely hated Touch the Sky for having grown up among the tribe's sworn enemies.

"Perhaps," Touch the Sky said coldly, still sitting his horse, "you would like to wager that I cannot do this thing again?"

Sparks of anger glinted in Wolf Who Hunts Smiling's dark eyes. But he only turned away, proudly saying nothing. In the beginning he had been free to mock and torment the newcomer at will. But since a special council had honored Touch the Sky's skill and bravery in saving the tribe from the Pawnee, his cousin Black Elk forbade such things. Nevertheless the cunning Wolf Who Hunts Smiling had eyes to see and ears to hear. Some in the tribe had been opposed to honoring Touch the Sky. And Black Elk, who loved Chief Yellow Bear's daughter, had noticed the long looks exchanged between Honey Eater and Touch the Sky. Wolf Who Hunts Smiling knew that Black Elk's forbearance would not last forever.

Touch the Sky, in turn, knew that his worst enemy was only biding his time. One night, shortly after their warrior training had begun, Wolf Who Hunts Smiling had deliberately stepped between Touch the Sky and the campfire, which was an Indian's way of identifying to others a person he intended to kill.

"My brother, too, was good with the ax," another Cheyenne youth said, glowering at Touch the Sky. The buck's name was Swift Canoe, and he blamed the tall outsider for the death of his twin brother True Son. And because True Son's body had been left in the camp of the tribe's enemy, it had not received a proper burial. As a result, his soul would wander forever in torment.

Touch the Sky held his face expressionless and refused to rise to the bait. Thanks to lies told by Wolf Who Hunts Smiling, many in the tribe believed that Touch the Sky had deliberately woken a Pawnee during a nighttime raid on their hidden camp. In fact it was Wolf Who Hunts Smiling who had caused True Son's death by disobeying Black Elk's orders—he had tried to take the scalp of the fierce Pawnee leader War Thunder. He had succeeded only in waking him up to raise the alarm.

"Enough!" Black Elk spoke coldly. "Hear these words and then place them in your sashes. Only women stand around and fight with their tongues! You will die in your sleep like old squaws, not gloriously like warriors!"

Without another word he handed the ax back to Little Horse. Touch the Sky's friend was smaller than the others, but sure in his movements like a good mountain pony. He was quiet, never boasting or complaining like Wolf Who Hunts Smiling and Swift Canoe. But the tribe knew well that behind Little Horse's quiet manner was a fierce fighter. He, too, had been honored for fighting bravely during the Pawnee raid on their camp.

Little Horse mounted his pony and successfully buried the ax deep into the cottonwood bark on his first pass. The fifth and last Cheyenne youth to try his skill was High Forehead, whose medicine bundle was the eagle's beak. The youngest of the group, he had been sent to train with Black Elk as a replacement for the dead True Son.

His first throw had range but missed the tree. When the ax stuck on the second throw, Touch the Sky and Little Horse offered brief words of praise. Then Black Elk ordered his entire band to mount.

He led them farther west until the tall grass began to give way to the short-grass prairie. To the southwest, the snowcapped peaks of the Bighorn Mountains reflected a pure white in the late-morning sun. The Cheyenne were one sleep's ride from Yellow Bear's camp on a grassy site halfway between the Powder and the Rosebud Rivers. It was the Moon When the Geese Fly South, and the days were still warm. Nights, however, were crisp with the promise of cold moons soon to come.

The young Indians practiced stringing and shooting arrows at a full gallop and charging in full battle rigs with streamered lances held high. Since being honored by the tribe, Touch the Sky was permitted to carry weapons. Before that time, Yellow Bear's people feared he might use a weapon against them. The Bowie knife at his waist and the Navy Colt pistol in his legging sash had been taken as trophies after he killed and scalped Hiram Steele's hired hand, who had tried to murder Touch the Sky when he returned to Bighorn Falls.

As the young Cheyenne entered the valley of the Rosebud to water their ponies, the cottonwoods grew thicker. Often the huge ridges in the bark of the trees were clotted with shaggy fur where passing buffalo had rubbed against it. Avoiding all wagon tracks, the youths swung wide to circle around a new fort with walls of squared-off cottonwood logs.

Suddenly, flocks of sparrow hawks and sand pipers rose from the river thickets in a panic and scattered. Black Elk raised his hand high, halting them. Their sister the sun was high in the sky. But an unnatural silence had settled over the valley like a heavy buffalo robe. Touch the Sky felt apprehension prickling in his blood.

"Dismount," Black Elk said tersely. "Tether your ponies and follow me."

"What is it, cousin?" Wolf Who Hunts Smiling said.

Black Elk sniffed the four directions of the wind. His fierce countenance became a mask of hatred. "White men!" he replied, and Touch the Sky and Little Horse exchanged worried glances.

All six Cheyenne dismounted and tethered their horses near the river with long strips of rawhide. They also removed the bright red Hudson's bay blankets and hid them in the thickets to avoid drawing attention to the spot.

Unconsciously, each of them fingered the pouch dangling from a buckskin thong on his breechclout. These were their medicine bags, which contained the special totem or magic object for each man's clan—feathers, claws, beaks, or precious stones. Touch the Sky's held a set of sharp badger claws Arrow Keeper, the tribe's medicine man, had given him.

"Attend to your weapons," Black Elk said.

Touch the Sky made sure he had a cap and cartridge in the loading gate of his pistol. When he looked up, Wolf Who Hunts Smiling was following him closely with his furtive stare. His dark eyes mocked Touch the Sky. In his hands, Wolf Who Hunts Smiling held a Colt Model 1855 percussion rifle that had once been Touch the Sky's. But when he was captured, a brave named War Bonnet took it from him and gave it to the younger Cheyenne.

Keeping his voice low so Black Elk would not hear, Wolf Who Hunts Smiling said, "Perhaps you would like to take it back, Woman Face?"

"It was rightfully presented to you by a warrior when I was a prisoner," Touch the Sky replied. "But it will be mine again."

Hatred forced the wily, mocking grin from Wolf Who Hunts Smiling's face. But before he could do anything, Black Elk, whose ears were keener than they thought, said angrily, "You two jays! Keep your chatter locked inside you and notice the language that matters!"

Following Black Elk's example, the rest scanned their surroundings in slow, careful sweeps of their heads. They moved forward slowly, knowing it was movement, not shape, that would catch an enemy's eye.

Soon Black Elk spotted something and knelt to examine the grassy bank of the river. Then he gathered the others around him and pointed to the tracks. "Iron hooves," he said. "White men's horses."

Black Elk showed them how to read the bend of the grass to tell how recently the tracks had been made. These were very fresh—the lush grass was still nearly pressed flat. A short distance along the bank, Touch the Sky and the others gaped in astonishment—the single set of tracks was joined by at least a dozen others!

They reached a huge dogleg bend in the river and worked their way through the thorny thickets in single file. The steady chuckle of the river helped to cover the sound of their passage. Touch the Sky emerged from the bend, following Little Horse, and cautiously poked his head around a hawthorn bush.

Several long moments passed before he could understand what he was seeing. When the enormity of it finally sank in, he felt hot bile rise in his throat. Only a supreme effort kept him from retching.

The scene was a comfortable river camp. There were several pack mules, one of them asleep over its picket. The hindquarters of an elk bull hung high in a tree to protect it from predators. Buffalo robes and beaver pelts were heaped everywhere, pressed into flat packs for transporting. The air was sharp with the pungent smell of castoreum, the orange-brown secretion of the beaver. Touch the Sky knew it gave off a strong, wild odor and was used by trappers as a lure to set their traps.

But what made his gorge rise were the three naked, hideously slaughtered white men in the middle of the camp.

All three had been scalped. They had also been castrated and their genitals stuffed into their mouths. Their eyes had been gouged out and placed on nearby rocks, where they seemed to stare longingly at the bodies they had once belonged to.

The camp was crawling with living white men, who were heavily armed. The strings of their fringed buckskins had been blackened by constant exposure to the blood of dead animals. And while Touch the Sky watched, one of them knelt beside a fourth dead man. Expertly, he made a cut around the top of the dead man's head. Then he rose, one foot on his victim's neck, and violently jerked the bloody scalp loose.

Touch the Sky looked away when the man castrated the corpse and gouged his eyes out with the point of his knife. The buckskin-clad man worked casually, as if he were digging grubs out of old wood.

The man turned toward him and Touch the Sky took a good look. Some instinct warned him this was a face he should know. The man was tall and thickset; he wore his long, greasy hair tied in a knot. When he turned, Touch the Sky saw a deep, livid gash running from the corner of his left eye well past the corner of his mouth.

The huge man with the scar appeared to be in charge. Occasionally he barked an order that Touch the Sky could not hear from that range. Whoever and whatever these men were, this slaughter appeared to be all in a day's work to them. One of the men was calmly boiling a can of coffee and mixing meal with water to form little balls. He tossed them into the ashes to cook. The leader casually scooped a handful out of the ashes and munched on them while his other hand still held the dripping scalp.

He barked out another command, and another of his men began folding beaver traps and lashing them to a pack mule. Only then did Touch the Sky become aware of all the whiskey bottles scattered throughout camp. Spotting more unopened bottles in cases lashed to the mules, the youth realized what had probably happened. The murderers had made their victims stuporous with strong water, then killed them in their sleep.

The scene was so horrible that Touch the Sky nearly cried out when a hand fell on his shoulder. But it was only Little Horse, showing him that Black Elk was signaling the retreat.

"There are too many and they are well armed. We must return to Yellow Bear's camp at once and report this in council!" Black Elk said as soon as they were out of earshot. "I care nothing if the paleface devils slaughter one another. But I fear a great storm of trouble will soon come—these killings were done so as to seem that red men did them!"

Chapter 2

During the rapid journey back to Yellow Bear's camp, Black Elk and his warriors-in-training were grim and raw nerved from what they had witnessed.

Black Elk had explained to his younger charges the seriousness of what they had just seen. Such ghastly mutilations of his earthly children were normally an offense to *Maiyun,* the Supernatural, and not the usual Indian way. Such a terrible death was reserved only for those guilty of especially horrible atrocities like mutilating war dead, raping women, or killing children. Furthermore, several Plains Indian tribes—the Arapahoe, the Shoshonee, the Gros Ventre, and the Sioux—were known to kill this way on occasion. But this was the heart of *Shaiyena* country, the Cheyenne homeland, and surely they would be blamed by other white men bent on revenge.

As they rode, Touch the Sky, Little Horse, and the oth-

ers remained silent and alert, using all their senses. Like
Black Elk, they constantly scanned the horizon, sniffed
the air, listened to every sound. But they spotted only
bighorn sheep and cougars in the higher elevations, and
one small buffalo herd down on the open plains. They
rode cautiously through scattered stands of scrub pine and
cedar, glimpsing mule deer and wolverines. Though they
strained their ears, they heard only the song of the lark,
the whistle of the willow thrush, the harsh calls of the hawk
and grebe.

When their sister the sun was halfway through her journey
across the sky on the day following the incident on the
Rosebud, Black Elk stopped his band beside a streamlet to
rest and water their horses. As usual, Touch the Sky and
Little Horse separated themselves from Wolf Who Hunts
Smiling and Swift Canoe. High Forehead, still not sure
of his place in the group, sat off by himself sharpening
his knife.

Wolf Who Hunts Smiling's furtive eyes followed Black
Elk until the warrior walked off to make water. Then he
slipped off to join him.

"Cousin," he said, "I have a thing to tell you."

Black Elk turned an impassive face to his young cousin.
True, the youth was strong and brave, and he feared death
less than a bird fears the air. But he was also rash and
foolhardy and prone to disobey orders. Black Elk remembered their raid, two moons ago, on a Pawnee mountain
stronghold. He strongly suspected that it was Wolf Who
Hunts Smiling, not Touch the Sky as his cousin claimed,
who had woken the Pawnee. In his zeal to scalp their
leader, he had brought revenge down on the camp of Yellow Bear.

"Speak this thing," he said coldly.

19

"Cousin," Wolf Who Hunts Smiling said, "it concerns Woman Fa—"

He caught himself just in time. "It concerns Touch the Sky and Honey Eater."

Black Elk's fiery black eyes grew slightly fiercer. Otherwise, his carved-in-stone face showed no reaction. "Speak!" he said again. "Or would you have me beg for gossip like girls in their sewing lodge?"

"I have seen them meeting together," Wolf Who Hunts Smiling said. This much was the truth. But now he added lies. "I have also heard him speaking against you. And Cousin, I have seen him hold Honey Eater in his blanket."

Still Black Elk showed no reaction, though his face felt as numb and dead as his sewn-on hunk of ear. His younger cousin was referring to a Cheyenne courting practice that had been adopted from the Dakota: a serious suitor would run up and throw his blanket around his chosen sweetheart, holding her fast while he spoke to her.

Despite his emotionless face, Black Elk felt a turmoil of feelings inside. True, Wolf Who Hunts Smiling hated Touch the Sky and did not always speak the straight word concerning him, but his cousin's story was consistent with something Black Elk had seen one night in the shadow of the medicine lodge. Touch the Sky and Little Horse had been honored earlier that day for saving the tribe from Pawnee raiders. That same night, Black Elk spied on Honey Eater and Touch the Sky, and he saw the chief's daughter cross her wrists over her heart—sign talk for love.

"I have no ears for these words!" Black Elk said scornfully. "How could Touch the Sky ever pay the bride-price for a chieftain's daughter? He marry Honey Eater? He who has no horses, no weapons, no meat, nor even a rack to dry it on? A fox will mate with an elk before she performs the squaw-taking ceremony with *him!*"

Wolf Who Hunts Smiling rejoiced at the anger in his cousin's tone. But he wisely refrained from further comment. As he rejoined Swift Canoe, he cast contemptuous eyes at the white men's scalps dangling from Touch the Sky and Little Horse's breechclouts.

"It takes no skill to raise the hide of dogs lying dead in the road," he said, looking at Touch the Sky. "I hear much of your bravery, but how is it that few in the tribe have witnessed these courageous deeds?"

Little Horse and Touch the Sky were seated side by side on a fallen cedar log, chewing on hunks of jerked buffalo.

It was Little Horse who answered. "You have cut me once," he said. "I still bear the scar on my chest from your knife. But pull a weapon on me again, and one of us will become worm fodder."

"Everything in its time," Wolf Who Hunts Smiling replied, still watching Touch the Sky.

"Yes," Touch the Sky agreed, recalling the night when his enemy deliberately stepped between him and the fire, thus making a clear death threat. "Everything in its own time."

Wolf Who Hunts Smiling only sneered scornfully and rejoined Swift Canoe. But oddly, his mention of the white men's scalps had set Touch the Sky to thinking of his life among the whites. Although Honey Eater had replaced his thoughts of Kristen Steele, the youth still fiercely missed his white parents. He knew they loved him and must be worried about him.

He also missed Corey Robinson and Old Knobby, the former mountain man who ran the Bighorn Falls Feed Stable. Corey had not hesitated for even the blink of an eye when Touch the Sky asked him to ride far into hostile Indian territory to help the tribe. And Old Knobby had saved his life when the Bluecoat lieutenant who was courting Kristen started to draw on him in rage after Touch the Sky had thrashed him.

Touch the Sky's reminiscences were put to an abrupt end by Black Elk's order to ride. Before the sun had lengthened their shadows much farther they had reached the grassy rise overlooking Yellow Bear's camp beside the Tongue River. The buffalo-hide tipis were pitched in clan circles, some spewing curls of cooking smoke out of their top holes. Nearby, a crude corral of buffalo-hair rope held the tribe's pony herd.

The lookouts had already spotted their approach. Now the camp crier raced throughout the village to announce their return. Touch the Sky had his own tipi beside Arrow Keeper's. Like Chief Yellow Bear's, theirs occupied a lone long hummock apart from the clan circles. Touch the Sky left his weapons in his tipi, then turned the dun loose with the herd to graze.

He knew the crier would soon be announcing a tribal council to discuss the incident on the Rosebud. But his muscles were still tense and his nerves raw from the things he had seen. He went down to a spot near the river where elk hides had been draped over a willow-branch frame to form a sweat lodge.

He stripped naked, slipped inside, and started a fire to heat a circle of rocks. When they finally glowed red hot, he poured cold water on them. The steam was so hot, at first, he could barely breathe it. But he could feel his muscles relaxing like a bowstring being slowly released. Gradually, the bloody images from the incident on the Rosebud River faded from his mind.

Then, as Arrow Keeper had taught him, he stepped outside and rubbed the glistening sweat off with clumps of sage.

This was followed by a cooling plunge in the river before he dressed again.

By the time he returned to his tipi the camp crier was announcing a council. Normally only the councillors— male representatives from each clan—and full warriors were allowed to attend. But the recent Pawnee raids had left Yellow Bear's tribe dangerously short of warriors. Since the junior warriors had fought bravely during the last raid, they were permitted to attend alongside the adult braves.

Touch the Sky donned beaded leggings decorated with feathers and his best moccasins adorned with porcupine quills. He stopped at Arrow Keeper's tipi, but the old medicine man had already left for the council. Touch the Sky joined the stream of men making their way toward the council lodge.

A huge square structure made of bent saplings with buffalo hides stretched over them, the council lodge dominated the center of camp. It had been painted red and tattooed with the secret and magic totems of the tribe. Nearby was the tribal scalp pole, displaying the hair of their enemies. One of the newest was the scalp of War Thunder, the Pawnee leader Touch the Sky had killed with a throwing ax during the raid on Yellow Bear's camp.

Seeing it made him pause and recall Wolf Who Hunts Smiling's taunting earlier that day. His pride in killing War Thunder was tempered by the knowledge that his act of skill had gone unwitnessed by all except Arrow Keeper and Honey Eater. As Arrow Keeper explained to him afterward, both witnesses would remain silent. Since many in the tribe resented the attention and friendship the two had shown him, their testimony would not be believed by all and would only further harden his enemies against him.

Touch the Sky was about to lift the flap and enter the

council lodge when he spotted a group of young girls walking together. They were on their way to the lodge where the tribe's unmarried women learned domestic arts from the squaws. One of the girls, white columbine petals braided through her long black hair, met his glance.

Touch the Sky felt his blood sing out at her beauty. Her frail cheekbones were high and finely sculpted, her bare legs like slender golden columns. The two of them exchanged a long look.

Suddenly a strong hand gripped his shoulder and roughly jerked him away from the entrance.

"Stand aside, mooncalf! This is a meeting of warriors!" said Black Elk. He had watched the exchange of looks with a fierce, disapproving glance in his dark eyes. "If you wish to learn cooking and beadwork, dress in a shawl and join your sisters."

His face warm with shame, Touch the Sky stood aside to let Black Elk enter. Then he went inside and joined the junior warriors seated against the back wall. The councillors sat in a circle in one half of the lodge. In their midst sat Chief Yellow Bear. He was wrapped in a red blanket, his silver hair flowing over his shoulders. At his left elbow sat Arrow Keeper, his ancient but distinguished face as weathered and wrinkled as an old apple core. He was older even than Yellow Bear, who counted 60 winters.

The other half of the lodge was filled with adult braves who were permitted to speak, but not to vote. As always, Chief Yellow Bear opened the council by filling his favorite clay pipe with a mixture of tobacco and red willow bark. He held it toward all the directions of the wind and smoked, then handed it to Arrow Keeper. The medicine man, in turn, passed it on to the headmen and the warriors. Touch the Sky, too, eventually took his turn.

Death Chant

After all had smoked, filling the lodge with the bittersweet fragrance of burning willow, Yellow Bear called for Black Elk to come forward.

"You saw me smoke this pipe," he said. "You have touched it with your own lips. Now unburden your heart and speak straight-arrow to your tribe."

"Father!" Black Elk said. "I am a warrior and will die the glorious death, not sleeping in my tipi. I have killed Pawnee and Crow and smeared the blood of my enemy on my face and arms. I have gone south and taken horses from the Kiowa and Comanche. I have counted coup on the Apache and Ute. But Father! These things I have seen recently on the Rosebud swell my heart with fear for your people!"

Yellow Bear and the rest listened attentively while Black Elk described the grisly murders that had been made to look like Indian treachery. Hearing it all again left Touch the Sky's heart racing, his palms slick with sweat. The moment Black Elk finished speaking, the lodge buzzed with excited and angry talk. Yellow Bear patiently folded his arms and the commotion quickly subsided.

"These words hurt my ears," Yellow Bear said. "No people are more terrible in their wrath for revenge than the white men." He turned to Arrow Keeper. "What is it you advise, shaman?"

"First," Arrow Keeper replied, "we must send word-bringers to all the Sioux, Cheyenne, and Arapahoe chiefs, informing them of this matter and learning what they may know of it. Then we must give a sun dance and cleanse our homeland of this foul thing."

"Fathers!" Black Elk said. "You are wise like the owl. These things are good and must be done, I agree. But they are not enough. We must also form a war party to track down and kill these treacherous whites!"

Again the lodge buzzed with talk. Chief Yellow Bear crossed his arms until the lodge was silent.

"Black Elk is a brave and strong warrior," Yellow Bear said, "and though he is young, he is our best battle chief. But he is quick to wade into the water before he can see the bottom. We know nothing of these white men. Who are they? What is their plan? Perhaps we can kill them, but will many more take their place and exact our blood for theirs?"

Many of the councillors approved this talk while some of the younger warriors were silent, supporting Black Elk. But before the debate could be carried farther, the flap over the door was suddenly lifted.

Surprised, Touch the Sky recognized a brave named River of Winds, whose medicine bundle was the rattlesnake. He was not at the council because he was the lookout at the northern approach to the camp.

"Fathers! Brothers!" he said, his voice tense with worry. "I ask your pardon for this interruption and for leaving my post. But I have important words for you!"

"Speak them," Yellow Bear said.

"You know that, three sleeps ago, Strong Eyes, Buffalo Hump, and Sun Road were sent with pelts to the trading post at Red Shale."

Yellow Bear nodded.

"All three of their ponies have returned," River of Winds said, "without their riders. And Buffalo Hump's pony is covered with blood!"

Chapter 3

Early next morning, even before the hunters left for the day, Touch the Sky made ready to ride out. Because he spoke the white man's tongue, he had been selected to accompany Black Elk and the other adult warriors to the trading post at Red Shale. Little Horse, whom Black Elk had witnessed fighting bravely during the Pawnee raid, was the only other junior warrior so honored.

Touch the Sky emerged from his tipi into the gray half-light of dawn. Dew still clung to the grass, and a low mist hung over the river like a pale ghost. Immediately he smelled elk steaks cooking and glanced over at Arrow Keeper's tipi. The old medicine man was cooking over the tripod just outside the entrance flap of his tipi.

"Eat," the shaman said when Touch the Sky walked over. He handed the youth a piece of bark that held a thick loin steak dripping kidney fat.

Arrow Keeper's cracked-leather face was lined deep with worry. "I have told you," he said while Touch the Sky ate, "of my vision at Medicine Lake. A dream was placed over my eyes, and in that dream I was told many important things about Yellow Bear's tribe. Soon I must speak to you more about this medicine vision."

Touch the Sky said nothing. His impassive face failed to reveal the strong emotions Arrow Keeper's vision always caused inside him. The old man was the keeper of the sacred Medicine Arrows, which were always renewed in a ceremony before battle. And Touch the Sky had seen proof of Arrow Keeper's big medicine. During the Pawnee attack he had thrown his magic panther skin over Honey Eater's shoulders, and even bullets fired point-blank failed to touch her.

"But now," Arrow Keeper said, "we face a new evil, and I fear for your safety. Before you ride out, bring me your pony."

Touch the Sky wanted to ask more, but knew he'd learn soon enough. He finished eating, rounded up the dun, and reported back to Arrow Keeper's tipi. The sun had still not cleared the crests of the Bighorn Mountains. Black Elk's party was just then assembling near Yellow Bear's tipi.

Using a lump of soft charcoal, Arrow Keeper drew magical symbols on the horse's flanks. He hung a medicine bundle from its hair bridle. Then he tied a polished antelope horn, into which he had inserted various herbs, around the pony's neck.

"Now," said Arrow Keeper, "join the others. I have just blessed your pony with long wind, speed, and strength."

Touch the Sky thanked him. By this time their sister the sun was starting to burn the mist off the river. Shortly thereafter Black Elk's party was riding toward the southernmost fork of the Powder. Their destination was the trading post at Red Shale, located just north of the soldiertown called Fort Connor. They hoped to discover Buffalo Hump, Strong Eyes, and Sun Road. Failing this, they hoped they could at least learn something of them.

It was a journey of one-and-a-half sleeps. They followed the river valley south, easily tracking the sign left by the three braves. Before their shadows were long in the sun on that first day, Black Elk rode up out of a cutbank and then immediately halted his pony. He stared hard at the trail before him. The others rode up beside him and also halted. For a long moment Touch the Sky, Little Horse, and the others stared, unable to move or speak.

The three missing Cheyenne lay dead across the trail, shot and scalped. Flies swarmed in thick, blue-black masses around the clotted blood. When Black Elk finally swung down off his horse, the others followed suit.

The bodies were riddled with lead, the popular .53-caliber buffalo balls used by white men. Except for the scalpings, no attempt had been made, such as had been done during the murders on the Rosebud, to make the deaths look as if they had been caused by Indians.

An empty travois lay beside the dead Cheyenne. It had once been piled high with buffalo and beaver pelts.

The sight shocked all of them to the core of their souls. Overcome with grief, a brave named Walking Coyote dropped to his knees beside his dead brother, Buffalo Hump. But he was a proud warrior and refused to let the grief come up from his heart into his face.

"I will burn down my tipi and cut short my hair," he said to the others, sorrow heavy in his voice. "All of my horses are for those who take them."

Surely his brother and the others had died before they could sing the death song. They would never cross over in peace to the Land of Ghosts. Instead, they must wander forever alone in the Forest of Tears, souls in pain. All Walking Coyote could do was sing a battle song to make the warriors' deaths less frightening.

"Only the rocks lie here and never move.
The human being vapors away."

The simple Cheyenne words made Touch the Sky's throat pinch shut. Even Black Elk, who despised public displays of feeling, was moved. For a moment he was forced to turn his face away. Though the ghastly scene saddened all of the Cheyenne, no one moved to stop Walking Coyote when he drew his knife and slashed his own arms.

While scarlet ribbons of Walking Coyote's blood trailed onto the ground, Black Elk lifted his voice in a vow. "Walking Coyote! Brothers! Hear me well. I know not who did this thing. Be they lice-eating Pawnee or white buffalo hunters, Ute or Crow, I swear by this battle lance they will die a hard death.

"Brothers, know this! They have no place to hide from Black Elk. If they be in breastworks, I will drive them out. I swear this thing to you, brothers!"

He held his streamered lance out and every buck present, including Touch the Sky and Little Horse, crossed his lance over Black Elk's. In that moment they were all red brothers, and all hatred between Touch the Sky and Black Elk was forgotten.

The bodies were lashed to the travois. Then Walking Coyote and a brave named Two Fists were sent back to camp with the dead. The others resumed their trek toward the trading post. Now they had to learn what they could about whoever sold the stolen pelts.

That night they camped in a copse beside Beaver Creek. The next day, when the morning sun was starting to burn warm, they crested the last rise before the trading post. Located on a crescent-shaped bend of the river, it was a long, square structure of cottonwood logs with oiled paper for windows and a slab door on leather hinges. Two pack mules, with huge panniers over their flanks for carrying goods, were tied to the rail out front. Beside them stood two saddle horses, a big sorrel and a claybank.

Black Elk watched the scene grimly. Unlike some of the headmen in the tribe, he was opposed to trading with the palefaces. True, ammunition, black powder, and tobacco were necessary things. It was foolish of the white man to part with such valuable items for beaver pelts and elkskins that any fool could obtain on his own.

It was also true that many of the traders tried to be good to Indians. After all, the red man brought them riches. But Black Elk never forgot that a soldier town stood nearby. There lived the long knives who killed the red man as casually as they might shoot prairie chickens.

"We will wait here," he announced to the others. "Touch the Sky will leave his weapons with us. He will ride down and speak with the whites. He will ask what they have heard about the killings. He will ask who has recently come with many beaver pelts and buffalo robes to trade."

Black Elk looked at Touch the Sky. "Be wary like the fox. The whites never speak the straight word to the red man. Watch to see if their eyes run from yours. Find the truth hidden behind their words."

Filled with pride at the responsibility, Touch the Sky held his face expressionless and only nodded. He nudged the dun and rode forward. While he dismounted in front of the trading post and tethered his pony, a fat, florid-faced white man was busy nailing a circular proclamation beside the door. Intent on his mission, Touch the Sky neglected to read it as he stepped inside. The fat man stared at him for a moment, his mouth dropping open.

Touch the Sky's moccasins were silent on the rough puncheon floor. The inside of the trading post was crowded and smelled of whiskey and leather and linseed oil. Everywhere he looked, various animal pelts had been pressed tight into standard packs for transportation back to the warehouses in New Orleans. The number in each pack varied according to the size of the animal: 10 buffalo robes, 14 bearskins, 60 otter pelts, 80 beaver, 120 fox, 600 muskrat. Four packs of beaver equaled 320 pelts and would fetch $700 at the post.

A bald, clean-shaven clerk in a paper collar glanced at Touch the Sky curiously for a moment. Then he turned back to wait on two customers who had heaved a pack of beaver pelts onto the broad deal counter. The clerk supplied them with two new rifles, cartridges, powder, coffee, sugar, and twists of chewing tobacco.

Both men were bearded and wore their filthy hair long. One, dressed in buckskins and a broad-brimmed plainsman's hat, turned sideways for a moment. Touch the Sky felt the back of his neck tingle when he recognized the coarse-grained face. It was the man he had seen at the camp on the Rosebud calmly cooking balls of meal while his leader scalped and mutilated a corpse!

He did not recognize the second man. Nor was there any sign of the scar-faced leader of the murdering band. Touch the Sky waited until the clerk had finished and the two men were gathering their supplies.

His tight-lipped mouth held as straight as a seam, he approached the counter. "I need some information," he said to the clerk.

All three men turned to stare, mouths agape.

"Christ Jesus!" the customer with the coarse skin said. "This white man has seen it all now, by beaver!"

"I don't credit it," his companion said. "Hell, he's one a them apple Injuns. Red on the outside 'n' white on the inside!"

Ignoring them, holding his face impassive, Touch the Sky asked the clerk the things Black Elk had told him to ask. He asked if there had been any word about the killing of three Cheyenne or if anyone had been in recently with a great number of buffalo robes and beaver pelts.

The clerk listened attentively. But when Touch the Sky finished speaking, the white man's eyes shifted toward the two filthy men. There was fear in the clerk's glance. Now Touch the Sky detected the strong odor of liquor on the breath of the two customers.

"Sorry, son," the clerk said. "I can't help you. I've heard nothing. We haven't had any buffalo hides come in for several days now." The clerk lowered his voice and added, "Do you know who that fat man out front is?"

Touch the Sky shook his head.

"He's from the Territorial Commission. You speak English good. Can you also read it?"

"Yes."

"Well, when you leave," the clerk said, "you best read that circular proclamation he's putting up." The clerk shot another glance at the grinning customers. "I had nothing to do with it, son. You tell your people that."

The coarse-skinned customer laughed. "Don't you fret, Harlan. Old fat Jacob ain't got the oysters to kill no Injun.

33

Everybody knows you're soft on the red Arabs since you took one as your reg'lar night woman."

He looked at Touch the Sky. "You got a set of stones on you, young buck, I'll give you that. Hell, it ain't been that long since you quit shittin' yellow. Now here you are, bold as a full-growed he-grizz, struttin' around in front of whites when there's a bounty on your dander."

His words confused Touch the Sky. Now the other customer said, "What tribe you with, boy?"

"Yellow Bear's."

The two men exchanged a long glance.

"Well, now," said coarse-skin, "that's mighty providential. We ain't had a chance to meet old Yellow Bear yet."

He stepped out front, then returned with a bottle of whiskey. "H'yar, take this to your big chief. Tell him it's a gift from my chief, Henri Lagace. Tell your people there's plenty more strong water where this come from."

When Touch the Sky backed up a few steps, refusing to accept the liquor, both men laughed.

"Well now," said the man Touch the Sky had seen on the Rosebud, "either you take this liquor, or me and Stone take your hair."

Seeing the confusion in the young Cheyenne's eyes, the clerk said, "Son, you best go read that circular."

Touch the Sky stepped back outside and read the official notice.

TO ALL WHO SHALL READ THIS NOTICE, GREETINGS. RECENT AND NUMEROUS ATROCITIES COMMITTED BY CHEYENNE INDIANS AGAINST WHITE TRAPPERS AND SETTLERS HAVE LED TO THIS PROCLAMATION: ALL CITIZENS, ACTING INDIVIDUALLY OR

IN SUCH PARTIES AS THEY MAY ORGANIZE, ARE HEREBY AUTHORIZED TO GO IN PURSUIT OF ALL CHEYENNE ON THE PLAINS. THEY ARE FURTHER AUTHORIZED TO KILL AND DESTROY, AS ENEMIES OF THE COUNTRY, ALL THAT CAN BE SEARCHED OUT. ALL MILITARY POSTS IN THE TERRITORY WILL ISSUE $20 IN GOLD FOR EVERY SCALP CERTIFIED TO BE CHEYENNE.

The words swam before his eyes, and Touch the Sky felt his face go numb. Suddenly, he understood the enormity of what the scar-faced leader and his murderous band were up to. By killing legitimate white trappers, they could profit from selling their furs. By making the deaths look Indian, they avoided any blame and made the Cheyenne the culprits. Thus, they could scalp Cheyenne for bounty—as they no doubt had done to Buffalo Hump and the others from Yellow Bear's tribe—and profit doubly. As if this treachery were not enough, they were stirring up more trouble by selling whiskey to the tribes.

The two white customers were grinning broadly when Touch the Sky, his thoughts still in a turmoil, came back inside. He knew he had to do something to stop this madness, but what?

"Please," he said. "This is wrong! Much trouble can be avoided if you speak to your leader. You must—"

"Whoa, blanket ass!" said the white called Stone. "You look as dry as a year-old cow chip. You swaller a swig or two o' this,'n' we'll hold palaver with you."

Touch the Sky was too desperate to refuse. The whiskey burned in a straight line to his gut and brought tears springing into his eyes. At the men's urging he swallowed another mouthful, then a third. Already his head felt light and the interior of the trading post began to blur.

"I don't hold with selling whiskey to Indians," said Harlan, the clerk. But he was silenced by a murderous stare from his customers.

One of the stinking whites threw his arm around Touch the Sky. The young Cheyenne was too confused to resist.

"Hell, Innun, we're your friends," said Stone. "You take the rest of this back to your chief 'n' tell him we got lots more to trade. If you wasn't our pard, you think we'd let twenty dollars in gold go unclaimed? A Cheyenne what speaks English can be right useful to us."

They said they were his friends. The room was spinning, and Touch the Sky felt his numb confusion giving way to a warm sense of inner peace. One of the men still had a friendly arm around him, both were grinning. Something had troubled him deeply only a moment before. But he forgot what it was. He was dizzy, but felt good. A broad, foolish smile broke out on his face. These men were not murderers, they were his friends, they—

"Touch the Sky!"

The words, spoken harshly in Cheyenne, shocked him out of his numb trance. He spun around and stared at the small, bronzed figure in the doorway.

"You are a white man's dog!" Little Horse said sharply. His dark eyes were filled with contempt. "We thought you were in danger, and Black Elk sent me down. Now I find you dancing and capering with the same paleface devil you saw committing murder only two sleeps ago. Wolf Who Hunts Smiling has been right all along—you are a spy for the whites!"

Chapter 4

Little Horse felt torn in his loyalties. He could not quite bring himself to report what he had seen to Black Elk. After all, Little Horse told himself, he had been wrong once before about Touch the Sky. He had accused him of trying to run away from battle with the Pawnee, when in fact he was only fleeing for help to save Yellow Bear's tribe.

Little Horse had been wrong before, but what he had just seen reawoke his distrust of his new friend. Touch the Sky had not only been drinking devil water with white men, but with one of the paleface butchers they had seen on the Rosebud! Now his friend was crazy from drinking and could barely mount his pony for the ride back to join the others.

By the time the youths had returned to the others, Touch the Sky had sobered enough to feel his face burning with shame. Black Elk and the other full warriors cast curious glances at the bottle in his hand when he and Little Horse rejoined the other warriors. Touch the Sky explained the message from the white men to Chief Yellow Sky. The warriors were troubled when Touch the Sky added that one of the whites had been involved in the Rosebud River slaughters. However, all else was forgotten when Touch the Sky explained about the white man's proclamation announcing a bounty on Cheyenne scalps.

Everyone was silent during the long ride back to the Tongue River village. His face stony with disapproval, Little Horse avoided all of Touch the Sky's glances. Each time his friend spoke to him, Little Horse pretended to hear nothing. He acted exactly as he had during the early days of their warrior training, when he had treated the new arrival's presence in camp as an embarrassment.

When they returned to the camp, they found the entire village in mourning for the three braves who had been killed on their way to the trading post. Several old squaws were keening in grief, and the warriors had all cut short their hair. The dead had already been outfitted in new elkskin moccasins for their journey to the Land of Ghosts.

Black Elk decided to take their news directly to Chief Yellow Bear instead of calling a tribal council first. With Touch the Sky at his side, they visited the old chieftain in his tipi. Reluctantly, Touch the Sky explained how he had drunk the strong water and become confused. He was surprised when the chief's leather-cracked face showed sympathy instead of anger.

"I have heard," Yellow Bear said, silver hair spilling out over his red blanket, "how the white men sometimes place bad medicine in their whiskey and rum to further the red man's need for it."

Yellow Bear explained how he had seen drunken red men snatch burning logs from the fire and rub them on their heads, rape buffalo cows, kill themselves and each other, freeze to death, drown, burn themselves up, and fall from their horses and break their necks.

When he finished speaking, the chief rose, took the bottle of whiskey outside, and dumped the contents out. He returned and listened with an impassive face while Touch the Sky again explained the message contained in the circular proclamation posted outside the entrance to the trading post.

"These words hurt my ears," he said when Touch the Sky had finished speaking. "Strong water is a danger to my people, but we can fight against those who would give it to us. However, how can we fight the entire white nation? For every paleface we kill, a swarm comes fighting. So long as this talking paper has power, anyone may kill Cheyenne."

After much meditation he sent Touch the Sky to find River of Winds, the same brave who had interrupted the last council to report on the three missing Cheyenne sent to the trading post.

"Select two good men," the Chief instructed River of Winds when the two had returned. "Learn from Touch the Sky just what these white men look like. Then wait near the trading post, well hidden, and watch for them. Follow them to their camp and learn about them. Then report to the council everything you have seen."

River of Winds nodded. After Touch the Sky had provided descriptions of the men he had seen, River of Winds left to carry out his orders. Yellow Bear, his aged face slack with worry, dismissed his visitors. Touch the Sky was returning to his tipi when he encountered Little Horse in the middle of the camp.

"Your eyes look through me as if I were not here," Touch the Sky said, his tone accusing. "Am I not your friend?"

"My red brothers," Little Horse replied stiffly, "do not caper and drink with white men's murdering dogs."

"Do you still call me a spy, then?"

Little Horse was slow to answer. "How can I know this thing? I have no eyes to stare into a man's heart and find his hidden secrets. It hardly matters. Even if you are not a spy, you do not hold the dignity of your tribe and your Indian blood in high honor. How can I trust a Cheyenne who plays up to palefaces? You have spent too much time among the whites, and now your blood calls out to be with them."

Touch the Sky felt heat rising into his face. "These words are foolish, I—"

"There is nothing else for me to say," Little Horse said, cutting him off. "From this time forward, I have no friend named Touch the Sky. My friends are Cheyenne, and Cheyenne do not play the dog for those who would kill them!"

With that Little Horse turned his back and walked away. Dejected, torn between anger and guilt, Touch the Sky returned to his tipi. There he used the bone-handle knife Arrow Keeper had given him to crop off his long black locks, honoring the three slain braves. Then he crossed to the old medicine man's tipi to discuss the troubling events of the past few days.

But the shaman had not yet returned from praying at the funeral scaffolds. Touch the Sky returned to his tipi once again. Exhausted, feeling more alone than he had since his early days with the tribe, he fell into a troubled sleep.

When he finally woke again, the meadow lark and the hermit thrush were making their melodious morning music. He sat up in his buffalo robes, fully awake. But when he glanced toward the entrance flap of his tipi, he was sure he must be dreaming.

Honey Eater was sitting there!

"Please," she said, her voice pleading with him to understand. "Do not think wrong things. There are things I must say to you. There is no other way I can speak with you."

She handed him a huge piece of bark filled with ripe serviceberries and juicy wild plums. But her troubled face told him this was not to be a social visit. He could smell the fresh white columbine braided through her hair. Her buckskin dress was adorned with beads, gold buttons, and shells.

"What is it that troubles you?" Touch the Sky said. He made no move to go nearer. He knew full well the punishment that would befall any unmarried Cheyenne man and woman caught together like this.

"Black Elk has sent his aunt, Sharp Nosed Woman, to my father with a gift of horses," she said, her eyes glistening with unshed tears.

Her news dug into Touch the Sky as if it were a knife turning inside his stomach. He had been with the tribe long enough to know the full significance of this act. Among the Cheyenne a marriage union was validated with an exchange of gifts. Acceptance by the girl's family of the first gift of horses, always sent through a female intermediary, bound the troth. Acceptance or rejection was expected by the first sunset.

"Did Yellow Bear accept this gift?" Touch the Sky said. The words felt like sharp thorns in his throat.

Normally, Cheyenne customs gave the prospective bride little choice in the matter. The decision of her father and brothers carried the most weight. Since Honey Eater had no brothers, and her mother had been killed in the Pawnee raid, the decision rested solely with Yellow Bear. However, the entire tribe knew that Honey Eater was the soul of the chief's medicine bag and that he doted on her. Therefore, her wishes would surely influence him to some degree.

"This time," she said, "the horses will be sent back. But I am not sure how many times this may be done before my father accepts them."

Touch the Sky understood her unspoken words too. She was hinting that tribal expectations would favor Black Elk. She could not keep persuading her father to send the horses back forever. Also, the tribe clearly did not fully accept Touch the Sky yet. He had no status, no possessions; he was still an outsider to many. It would be a terrible affront to the tribe if he set his sights on the daughter of a chief.

In short, she was pleading with Touch the Sky to become somebody in the eyes of the entire tribe, and to do so quickly. Otherwise she would have to marry Black Elk. The betrothal was supposed to be accompanied by a feast, a great giving away of goods that corresponded to the girl's status. Honey Eater was the daughter of a great peace chief. The impossibility of his situation filled Touch the Sky with hopeless desperation.

"Black Elk is a warrior," he said miserably. "A war chief despite his young age. Only a warrior can court and marry."

Despite his bravery so far, Touch the Sky was not an official warrior. He had never taken part in the Medicine Arrows ceremony nor gone to war as Black Elk had. Thus he could not throw his blanket around any tribal female and grab her for love-talk unless he had also first seized and stopped an enemy in battle.

Also, unlike Black Elk, Touch the Sky had not earned even his first eagle feather. Black Elk boasted many in his warbonnet. These meant that he had counted coup on an enemy. Even more honorable than killing an enemy in battle was to strike him with quirt, bow, or knife before he actually attacked. This symbolic strike caused no injury and said to the enemy, "I have deliberately not killed you yet, giving you a chance to strike me first. See how brave I am, how little I fear you!"

Realizing there was nothing more to discuss, Honey Eater rose and said, "I must leave now."

Only then did Touch the Sky finally move, accompanying her to the flap. As if they both silently understood the possible danger of touching each other in such intimate quarters, Touch the Sky only allowed himself to briefly touch her fragrant black hair with his lips. Then she lifted the flap, peered carefully outside, and left.

For a moment Touch the Sky gazed after her, watching the delicate swaying motion of her slim hips as she walked. He was about to close the flap again when he spotted something that made his blood run cold.

Partially hidden behind Arrow Keeper's tipi, watching him with savage hatred in his usually stoic face, was Black Elk.

He must have followed Honey Eater when she came, Touch the Sky realized with a grim sense of foreboding. Black Elk was making life miserable enough for him as it was. Now, seeing Honey Eater leave his tipi on the same day when his marriage gift would be returned, what would his wrath be like? Touch the Sky suspected that Black Elk would not report this forbidden visit to the tribe elders at council. It was the fierce warrior's way to settle his own scores.

Black Elk cast him a final, malevolent glance, then turned and stalked away. Touch the Sky was about to drop the flap again when suddenly the pounding hooves of the camp crier's pony caught his attention.

"A word-bringer has arrived!" he shouted over and over. "A word-bringer from the Lakota!"

The arrival of a word-bringer from the Sioux was a great event. Touch the Sky hurried to join the people milling toward the council lodge in the middle of camp. The word-bringer had already arrived. He was too excited to wait for the usual formalities of smoking to the four directions.

"Yellow Bear!" he shouted as soon as the old chief arrived. He pointed west across the river. "Over there two sleeps! Five Cheyenne hunters have been found dead in their camp. All have been scalped and mutilated. And all are from Yellow Bear's tribe!"

Chapter 5

Despite the serious news about the five dead Cheyenne hunters, the headmen delayed their council. They followed Yellow Bear's advice to wait until the scouts he had sent out returned.

However, the incident made the entire tribe fully aware of the danger they faced. Extra sentries were posted at the approaches outside of camp, and hunting parties were temporarily suspended. Only braves leading warriors in training were allowed to ride out. The headmen agreed with Yellow Bear that, more than ever, it was necessary to provide the tribe with capable fighters to defend them.

On the morning after the Sioux word-bringer arrived, Black Elk gathered his party and led them northwest toward the Little Bighorn River. It was rumored that their enemies, the Crow, were hunting in that area. Crow raiding parties had recently stolen ponies from Cheyenne herds in daring nighttime raids. Now Black Elk had his mind set on revenge.

One sleep after they had set out, riding hard, Black Elk called a rest at midday. Once again Touch the Sky found himself sitting alone, as he had in the early days of training. He was not surprised when Black Elk approached him, his face grim with hatred. Only the night before, Black Elk's ponies had been returned from Honey Eater.

"Do you see this?" he said, pointing to the dead flap of leathery skin where his detached ear had been sewn on. "A Bluecoat saber took it off. But the soldier who did it paid with his life. I told you before that I never give up anything that is mine without a fight to the death.

"The entire village knows by now that my horses have been sent back. This thing humiliates Black Elk. You and I alone know why the horses were sent back. You have plotted against me. You have whispered the love words that have confused Honey Eater's mind."

"No!" Touch the Sky said. "Not once have I done these things!"

"Silence! When a warrior speaks, a child listens! There was a time when my heart began to change toward you. Truly, you have worked hard and made great progress. I no longer consider you the worthless white dog you seemed at first. You are strong and capable, and I believe there is courage in your heart."

Despite his anger at the unjust charge, Touch the Sky felt a warm glow of pride at this rare recognition from the warrior.

"However," Black Elk said, "we must be enemies from this day forth. I am a man of honor and will not let my emotions lead my heart. I will not treat you unjustly nor value your life less than that of the others. But know that there must come a time when Honey Eater either accepts my horses or you and I must fight to the death. Do you understand this?"

After a long pause, Touch the Sky nodded. Again misery and loneliness filled his heart. Following Little Horse and Wolf Who Hunts Smiling's lead, the rest were ignoring him. Now Black Elk was telling him that if he persisted in his love for Honey Eater, he was a dead man. Would acceptance never come?

"Good," Black Elk said. "Now prepare to ride."

Again they pointed their horses toward the Little Bighorn country. As they crossed a wide stream, they spotted an elk buck about to cross downstream from them. Black Elk showed them how to wait until a target was thigh deep in the water before attempting to kill it, thus slowing it down in case a second shot was needed. He brought it down with his first shot. Then they dressed out the meat and packed it along with them.

With every member of Black Elk's band fully aware of the talking paper back at the trading post, a sense of danger followed them every moment. The white men had always been their enemies. But now Cheyenne scalps were worth gold.

The band encountered a huge buffalo wallow just outside the tableland overlooking the Little Bighorn. The muddy depression was filled with tufts of buffalo hair and fresh tracks, where Indian ponies had skirted the edge. Black Elk studied the tracks for a long moment and then pointed out the slight cleft made by the back of the hooves—the distinctive mark of the stocky mountain breed preferred by Crow hunters and warriors.

Black Elk pointed toward a gama-grass meadow high up on the foothills, just below the rimrock of the Little Bighorn

Mountains. "We must ride up to the high country," he said, "and spot our enemy first before we ride farther."

They rode single-file through a huge stand of aspen, then up a narrow defile. As they approached the meadow, Wolf Who Hunts Smiling turned to cast his furtive, hateful stare at Touch the Sky. The look was a reminder that Wolf Who Hunts Smiling had vowed to kill him. Now, with Swift Canoe and Little Horse his enemies and even High Forehead ignoring him, Touch the Sky felt a sense of apprehension like a tight knot in his belly. Once he had heard old Arrow Keeper say that a Cheyenne without friends was a dead man. These thoughts were soon forgotten, however, when Touch the Sky and the others reached the meadow and obtained a good view of the river valley below.

"There!" Black Elk said, pointing toward a cliff with limestone outcroppings overlooking the river. "The Absaraka!"

He had used the ancient name of the Crow, who normally hunted in the Yellowstone Valley. Below, five Crow braves had gathered around a fire to roast fresh-killed buffalo. Their horses were tethered in the lush grass at the edge of the river. The Crow tribe had lately begun to move farther west from the Yellowstone to the mountains the whites called the Rockies. Now there were the River Crow and the Mountain Crow.

"Stub-hands," Black Elk said with contempt. This was a mocking reference to the Crow practice of chopping joints off their fingers as a sign of mourning. Sometimes a group of braves did not have a whole hand among them. Warriors would save their thumbs and trigger fingers.

"We will attack," Black Elk said, "and we will steal the horses. But we will not draw the blood of our enemies. The Stub-hands have stolen our ponies, but it has been many moons since they have sent any Cheyenne under. Only the lice-eating Pawnee kill when it is not necessary to do so. The Cheyenne kill only in self-defense or for revenge when our people are killed. We will do something braver than killing: we will count coup."

Among the Crow, any horses seized by a raiding party belonged to the leader. He was then expected to divide them among the party as an act of generosity. But the Cheyenne, Black Elk explained, believed that any horse belonged to whichever brave first struck coup on it by touching it in his first pass. The brave with the fastest horse was thus at a great advantage.

At this, Touch the Sky and Wolf Who Hunts Smiling exchanged long stares. Though Wolf Who Hunts Smiling was considered the best rider in Black Elk's party, Touch the Sky's spirited dun was the swiftest pony.

"When we draw nearer," Black Elk said, "select the pony you wish to own. Then ride like the wind, count coup in your first pass, and seize it by its hackamore during your second pass. Then flee back here toward the high country. Cheyenne honor demands that you select another horse if you witness another Cheyenne touch the pony before you."

This last remark was directed at Wolf Who Hunts Smiling and Touch the Sky. Then, once again leading his warriors-in-training in single file, Black Elk retraced their path back down toward the river valley.

Hugging the south bank of the river, well hidden by thickets and thick stands of cottonwood, the Cheyenne approached slowly until they reached an elbow bend just before the Crow campsite. The water was shallow there and they crossed easily. Black Elk fanned them out in a skirmish line, taking the lead. He raised his hand. Touch the Sky felt his throat tightening and his heart scampering in his chest like a frenzied animal. Soothingly, he stroked the dun's neck and spoke softly to her.

Black Elk plunged his hand down. *"Hiya, hi-i-i-ya!"* he screamed, and hearing the war cry, Touch the Sky felt his blood humming in his veins.

The band of Cheyenne broke around the bend, riding six abreast, and completely surprised the Crow hunters. Immediately Touch the Sky saw the pony he wanted: a spotted gray with a beautiful white mane. He dug his heels into the dun's flanks and surged ahead of the others.

But a moment later, in the corner of one eye, he was aware of Wolf Who Hunts Smiling's pure black pony about to catch up to him. Wolf Who Hunts Smiling was riding in classic Cheyenne fashion, swung low over his pony's neck to present a small target.

The first surprised Crow were running for their rifles, stacked halfway between the fire and their horses. Suddenly, Wolf Who Hunts Smiling swung deftly from his pony's left flank to the right, kicking out with his right foot. Touch the Sky felt a painful blow to his temple, saw a burst of bright orange light inside his skull as his enemy almost kicked him off his dun. But somehow he managed to cling to her, urging her forward even faster.

A rifle spoke its piece, another, and Touch the Sky heard a noise like an angry hornet as a bullet whizzed past his ears. There were more shots, and abruptly High Forehead's pony collapsed. Wheeling his horse almost in mid-stride, Little Horse abandoned the ginger buckskin pony he had been about to count coup on. He raced back and took the fallen Cheyenne up behind him. Knowing it was useless to attempt a coup now, Little Horse raced back toward the high country.

Touch the Sky was bearing down rapidly on the gray, his own horse about a half-length ahead of Wolf Who Hunts

Smiling's black. He leaned sideways, struck with his right hand, and felt solid contact. A moment later Wolf Who Hunts Smiling also struck coup. Touch the Sky wheeled his dun, bullets buzzing all around him now, and seized the gray's buffalo-hair hackamore. He broke for the gama-grass meadow.

Cursing him, Wolf Who Hunts Smiling counted coup on a roan pony and followed him. Black Elk brought up the rear, leading a huge claybank.

Swift Canoe was the only casualty of the raid. He had caught a slug in his right thigh and been forced to flee without counting coup. In all, they had seized three ponies, enough to persuade the Crow that it was useless to attempt to follow them. Black Elk praised his party for their bravery, singling out Little Horse for saving High Forehead when his pony was shot out from under him.

"Not one of you showed the white feather," he said. "My heart swells with pride!"

"But cousin!" Wolf Who Hunts Smiling said in protest. "Touch the Sky has stolen my horse! I first counted coup on the gray, but he seized it on his first pass while I was making my second, as you instructed."

Black Elk's face hardened, his black eyes were like two hard agates. He rode forward until he was directly in front of the two younger Cheyenne.

"Does my young cousin speak straight-arrow?" he demanded of Touch the Sky.

"He speaks in a wolf bark, living up to his name," said Touch the Sky. "I first struck coup."

The usual way to settle such disputes was to rely on a witness. "Did anyone else see what happened?" Black Elk said.

No one spoke up. Touch the Sky felt his heart sink. Black

51

Elk hated him, and he had not even one friend in the group. Surely he would lose this magnificent animal!

A moment later he gasped in shock when Black Elk roughly shoved Wolf Who Hunts Smiling off his black. The young Cheyenne landed hard on his back.

"I saw what happened," Black Elk said angrily to his fallen cousin. "I saw you attempt to knock Touch the Sky from his horse, and I saw him strike coup first. Know this. My heart is like a stone toward Touch the Sky. I care not if he lives or dies. But a Cheyenne warrior's honor demands that he must always speak the straight word about counting coup. Touch the Sky performed like a true brave, and the gray is his. As punishment for your lies, you will present your stolen horse to High Forehead to replace his dead pony."

Wolf Who Hunts Smiling started to protest, but Black Elk silenced him with a withering stare. Touch the Sky's heart swelled with joy. But Black Elk turned to him and, keeping his voice low so the others could not hear, said, "You remember what I told you. Either Honey Eater accepts my horses, or you and I must fight to the death."

Soon after Black Elk's group returned to the Tongue River camp, Chief Yellow Bear and the headmen called a council.

River of Winds and the braves he had selected had returned from the scouting mission ordered by Yellow Bear. As the councillors and warriors assembled in the huge central lodge, a sense of urgency filled everyone.

When Touch the Sky entered the lodge, no one acknowledged his presence. High Forehead started to nod. Then he saw how Little Horse had turned his head, and he did the same. But as Touch the Sky took his place along the back wall with the other warriors-in-training, old Arrow Keeper looked up from the pipe he was preparing. He nodded at the tall, broad-shouldered youth. His heart surging in gratitude, Touch the Sky nodded back.

Arrow Keeper passed the pipe to Chief Yellow Bear. The old silver-haired chief, his worried and weary face as lined as dry riverbed clay, smoked to the four directions. He passed the pipe on to the headmen. Soon the smell of burning red willow bark filled the lodge. Yellow Bear then called on River of Winds to make his report.

River of Winds was of medium height and slender build. His rich black mane of hair had been cropped short in mourning for the three braves killed on their way to the trading post and the five dead hunters reported by the Lakota word-bringer.

"Fathers! Brothers!" he said after taking his place next to Yellow Bear in the center of the lodge. "We are up against an evil and powerful enemy. I, Scalp Cane, and Porcupine Bear hid ourselves on the ridge overlooking the paleface trading post. Soon we saw the two palefaces described by Touch the Sky bearing beaver pelts to the post.

"We followed them for nearly two sleeps, until they reached a huge camp near the Knife River just west of Mandan country. Here we saw many whites, some appearing to live in the camp, many more reporting in small groups from outlying camps. We also saw the scar-faced white leader whom Black Elk spoke of—the leader of the butchers at the Rosebud camp.

"Fathers! Brothers! Hear my words now and place them forever near your heart, for they are true words and sad words. The whites returning to this central camp bore not only furs and pelts, but the scalps of our red brothers. We followed the ugly scar-face and several of his men. The things we saw were not meant for the eyes of men who believe in the Great Spirit. We saw these palefaces give devil water to their own white brothers, and then, when they had made them senseless with drink, raise their hair while they slept!"

River of Winds paused, fighting to regain control of his emotions. It was not right to show his feelings before this assemblage of wise men and warriors. But the things he had seen had smitten his heart like the blade of a tomahawk.

"We also saw this team of white murderers encounter a small group of Cheyenne belonging to the band led by Shoots Left-Handed. Again the scar-face plied them with strong water and scalped them in their drunken sleep. And this time the scalps were taken to the soldiertown the whites call Fort Grand. We were not able to follow closely, but when the palefaces emerged from the fort, they no longer had the scalps of our *Shayiyena* brothers."

River of Winds turned his face for a moment until he was under control again. Then he concluded, "Fathers! Brothers! We were not painted for battle and had made no sacrifice to the sacred Medicine Arrows. Had we done these things, we would have died trying to defend our Cheyenne brothers. But Yellow Bear ordered us to observe only and to report what we had seen. Never will I forget this terrible thing I have witnessed, nor forgive myself that I did not fight like a man to prevent the bloodshed of our own!"

He finished speaking and returned to his place among the warriors. For a long time Yellow Bear was silent, his weathered face impassive. The cold moons would soon be approaching, and there was a knife edge of chill in the air. He pulled his red blanket tighter about his shoulders. Finally he spoke, his voice heavy with sadness.

"Brothers! Your chief has rinsed his mouth in cold, fresh

water, and now he speaks only true things. There is none among us who hates war and killing more than I. Young men dream of glory, of counting coup and taking scalps. Old men desire only a warm fire and a full belly.

"Twice now have I lost good wives to our enemies. The sadness in my heart is big like the plains, and were it not that my people need me, I would fall on my knife and join my wives in the Land of Ghosts. But the things that River of Winds has told us today have turned my heart into a stone. There is no soft place left in it. Now your chief says this. Warriors, ready your battle rigs! We will dance the war dance and make our sacrifices to the Medicine Arrows. Arrow Keeper, how do you counsel?"

The old medicine man rose and spoke without hesitation. "I back my chief in this thing. This evil scar-face and his white murderers must be stopped. There is a bounty on Cheyenne scalps, and we are targets for all who would profit from our death. Now these white dogs are killing our people. And it will not stop with this. Soon these white dogs will turn Cheyenne against Sioux, Jicarilla against Ute. Their strong water will divide the red nations and weaken us against our white enemies."

These words were met with unanimous shouts of approval.

"Then it is decided," Yellow Bear said. "It is time for Yellow Bear, your peace chief, to pray and meditate and seek medicine visions. From this time forth, you follow Black Elk, your war leader. Arrow Keeper! Make ready the sacred arrows. Until these white dogs are hunted down and destroyed, the Cheyenne are at war!"

Chapter 6

Only one sleep after the war council was held, Arrow Keeper sent the crier throughout camp, announcing to all blooded warriors and warriors-in-training that a sacred Medicine Arrows ceremony would be held later.

The war dance and offering to the arrows would take place soon after the sun had hidden herself under the western horizon. When his shadow began to lengthen, Touch the Sky gathered with the rest of the tribe in the open area before the council lodge. Black Elk, their official war chief, had called all men, women, and children together before the ceremony. It was his duty as war leader to explain his strategy for fighting the treacherous white murderers who were posing as traders and trappers.

The cold moons were not far off, and a crisp chill stiffened the breeze. Occasionally, dead leaves were stripped from the cottonwood trees bordering the river and fluttered down among the gathering clans. Most of the men had abandoned their light breechclouts for buckskin shirts and leggings.

"Cheyenne people!" Black Elk shouted, standing on a tree stump so he would rise above the others. He was fierce in his crow-feather warbonnet. "Have ears for my words!"

The hubbub of conversation ceased. Touch the Sky felt eyes on him and glanced to his right. Little Horse was staring at him from nearby, suspicion etched into every feature.

Pointedly, making sure Touch the Sky saw him, Little Horse averted his eyes. He moved farther away until he was lost in the crowd. Touch the Sky felt heat rising into his face at the snub. He had lost his last friend in the tribe except for Arrow Keeper and Honey Eater— and she had to keep her feelings secret from the others.

Why, Touch the Sky berated himself again, had he been foolish enough to drink the paleface strong water and let the murderers pretend to be his friends? His mistake had convinced Little Horse that he was a white man's dog, not a true Cheyenne among Yellow Bear's people.

"Cheyenne!" Black Elk said. "This time our enemies are not the lice-eating Pawnee, who attack us where we live and attack as one people. Our enemies are wily as the fox, slippery as the weasel. And like wolves worrying a buffalo herd, they divide into packs for the kill!

"Therefore, we, too, will fight in packs. We will follow the scar-faced leader's teams. They are well armed with new rifles and abundant ammunition. We are short of black powder and lead. But we will hunt them out, hound them, and kill or drive them from our lands. Let them hide in forest or cave, let them flee into the mountains—their scalps will dangle from our lodgepoles, or may Black Elk die of the yellow vomit!"

Three times he thrust his red-streamered lance high over-head. Three times the warriors shouted their approval of his brave oath.

"Warriors!" Black Elk said. "Now our sister the sun flees from the sky. Return to your tipis and ready your battle rigs. Paint your faces for war. Prepare to sing, to dance, to make your offering to the sacred arrows!"

Another shout greeted his words. Soon the square was emptying as everyone hastened to prepare.

Lost in thought, Touch the Sky had almost reached the flap over his tipi before he noticed two figures in the grainy twilight of early evening—Swift Canoe and Wolf Who Hunts Smiling.

Arrow Keeper had packed tobacco and balsam into Swift Canoe's leg wound and wrapped it with strips of soft cedar bark. The young Cheyenne still blamed Touch the Sky for the death of True Son, his twin brother, in the mountain stronghold of the Pawnee. But Touch the Sky knew the blame lay with Wolf Who Hunts Smiling. Too eager for a scalp, Wolf Who Hunts Smiling had woken War Thunder, the Pawnee leader, and thus alerted the entire camp. True Son had been shot while trying to escape.

But the malice in Swift Canoe's face was nothing compared to the fierce hatred in Wolf Who Hunts Smiling's furtive eyes. "Woman Face!" he said with contempt. "You have stolen my gray pony. I first counted coup, and now that horse should be mine."

Although Touch the Sky towered over the smaller Cheyenne, he was wary. Wolf Who Hunts Smiling could strike as swiftly as a rattlesnake. "You are without shame or honor," Touch the Sky said. "It is bad enough that you speak with two tongues in front of the others. But to lie now, looking into my eyes, when you saw me count coup first. There is nothing good in your heart. You are a disgrace to your tribe."

Wolf Who Hunts Smiling's wily face twisted with rage. In a moment his knife was in his hand.

Despite Wolf Who Hunts Smiling's vow to kill him, Touch the Sky knew even then that his enemy would not kill him in camp. Cheyenne law demanded that any Cheyenne killing another be ostracized, even in cases of accidental death. The killer was not usually banished from the tribe—such a fate was so horrible, to an Indian, that even murderers were spared this punishment. But murderers and their families were banned from participating in the Medicine Arrows ceremony. The ceremony, also known as the renewal of the arrows, was not just important as a battle ritual—it provided the main deterrent to murder within the tribe since the killing of one Cheyenne by another bloodied the sacred arrows. And bloodying the arrows thus endangered the well-being of the entire tribe.

Nonetheless, Wolf Who Hunts Smiling loved to cut with his blade, and Touch the Sky knew this. He also knew that his enemy liked to rely on the element of surprise. Touch the Sky had learned the hard way not to lose this advantage. Now he moved quickly.

Knowing full well Swift Canoe would jump him too, Touch the Sky reached into his legging sash and drew out his Navy Colt. In the same motion with which he drew it out, he flung it hard at Swift Canoe's head. There was a harsh thud as the heavy weapon cracked Swift Canoe in the forehead. His breath escaping in a surprised hiss, he crumpled unconscious to the ground.

An instant later Touch the Sky leaped backward, barely missing the point of Wolf Who Hunts Smiling's blade as it slashed in front of his chest. A moment later Touch the Sky's

Bowie was in his hand, and he leaped forward before the other Cheyenne could recover his balance from his missed attempt.

Touch the Sky slashed down hard diagonally, opening a wound from Wolf Who Hunts Smiling's right shoulder to his left ribcage. The wound was not deep, but instantly rivulets of blood were pouring down his front and dripping into the ground.

Wolf Who Hunts Smiling cried out in shock at the white-hot pain. His knife fell from his hand. Touch the Sky kicked it off into the brush around them.

"There!" Touch the Sky said triumphantly. "I have counted coup twice before your eyes! Will you still lie and tell me you struck first?"

Despite his pain and humiliation, Wolf Who Hunts Smiling's swift eyes never once left his enemy. He was livid with hatred.

"Enjoy your victory, white man's dog! Your days with this tribe are numbered. Even Little Horse, once your shadow, has turned against you. Now Black Elk's horses have been returned by Honey Eater, and everyone knows why! Strut now, Woman Face! The day comes when your guts will be carrion for the buzzards and coyotes!"

With that, Wolf Who Hunts Smiling knelt to revive Swift Canoe. Not turning his back until he was well away, Touch the Sky returned to his tipi to prepare for the renewal of the arrows. But the elation of his victory was tempered by the truth of his enemy's words.

Arrow Keeper was deeply troubled.

He had fought many enemies in his time and seen many trials and much sadness. Once, many winters ago when he was still a warrior, the sacred arrows had been captured by

Pawnee. Until the arrows were again recovered, those were perhaps the blackest days for the Cheyenne people.

But this new danger, he thought as he rummaged underneath his buffalo robes, was an enemy no red man knew how to fight. White men and devil water—the strong water could destroy a tribe faster and more completely than Bluecoat canister shot.

The ceremony would begin soon, and he had already donned his special calico shirt painted with magic symbols. His face was greased as the warriors would grease theirs on the warpath. His forehead was painted yellow, his nose red, his chin black. His single-horned warbonnet contained 40 feathers in its tail, one for each time he had counted coup against an enemy.

He removed the coyote-fur pouch that contained the arrows. But he held them without unwrapping them, still lost in pensive thought.

There were more and more reports about strong water reaching the surrounding Indians. Strong water made the red men crazy and destroyed their belief in *Maiyun,* the Supernatural. Thus it also eroded their warrior courage and virtue.

Arrow Keeper knew that the Great White Father, who lived far east of the river called The Great Waters, had tried to do right. He had spoken to his white headmen and they had passed laws meant to help the Indians. Traders were required to buy talking papers called licenses and were not legally permitted to sell alcohol to red men inside Indian territory.

There were also laws, more talking papers, which declared that white squatters within Indian territory were to be evicted by Bluecoats. But all these laws were ignored. Nowhere could a white man's council—called a jury—be found that would convict whites in cases involving Indians.

His heart heavy with a sense of foreboding, Arrow Keeper unwrapped the coyote-fur pouch. Four stone-tipped arrows, dyed bright blue and yellow and fletched with scarlet feathers, lay inside.

"May they bring the tribe strong medicine," he prayed. Protecting those four arrows was his chief tribal responsibility. For this great honor he was called Arrow Keeper and allowed to preside over the sacred Medicine Arrows ceremony. The fate of these four arrows represented the fate of the tribe.

The Medicine Arrows were the equivalent of the white man's Bible. Whenever a Cheyenne swore a sacred oath, he did so while touching a buffalo skull on which were painted four arrows. The Keeper of the Arrows was considered so important and holy that he could not be deposed or subjected to Cheyenne law. The only other Cheyenne so honored were tribal chiefs and the chiefs of the soldier societies such as the Dog Soldiers and the Bowstrings.

It was Arrow Keeper's sacred job to keep the arrows forever sweet and clean. But it was also each member of the tribe's responsibility to keep them from defilement. Arrow Keeper knew the renewal of the arrows ceremony was important because it reminded each Cheyenne that he was closely linked to the tribe. It made him mindful of his fellow men and more respectful of their rights, as well as more likely to fulfill his obligations. Quarreling and even undue noises were forbidden during the ceremony. Though only warriors would participate in that night's battle ceremony, the entire tribe took part in the annual renewal.

He lifted the elkskin flap of his tipi and saw that night had drawn her black shawl over the camp. Far-flung stars blazed like gems in the vast dark dome of the sky. Bright fires were lit throughout the camp, including the huge one near the council lodge, flaming bright in preparation for the renewal of the arrows.

The old man watched all of it for a moment, his painted, weather-lined face like a grotesque and ancient mask in the flickering light. Once again his thoughts veered toward the tall Cheyenne youth called Touch the Sky.

The young buck had made amazing progress since his first stumbling, halting days with the tribe. He had even been honored in a special council. But now he was in trouble again. Arrow Keeper had sensed it when Black Elk's scouting party returned from the trading post. Touch the Sky and Little Horse were no longer friends. Worse, Touch the Sky had earned the wrath of the jealous and dangerous warrior Black Elk. Black Elk was a warrior of honor, but he was covered with hard bark and determined to get his way. His sense of honor would not let him be humiliated by a junior warrior—even one who had counted coup successfully and was about to participate in his first Medicine Arrows ceremony.

But again the old shaman reminded himself that he had seen with his own eyes the mulberry-colored birthmark hidden behind Touch the Sky's hairline. It was in the shape of an arrowhead—the mark of the warrior. Touch the Sky was surely the young Cheyenne of his medicine vision, the son of a great chief and the savior of the *Shaiyena*.

Arrow Keeper left his tipi, the arrows tucked carefully under one arm, and crossed camp to join the growing circle around the fire.

Already the drummers were beating a hypnotic rhythm on huge hollow logs. The blooded warriors had already assembled, faces painted like Arrow Keeper's. They carried their decorated shields and wore their crow-feather warbonnets. As always, Honey Eater and a young girl from the Crooked

Lance Clan were serving as maids of honor at the ceremony. They kept time with stone-filled gourds while the warriors took turns dancing with their knees kicking high. Beaded buckskins and brightly painted faces glinted in the firelight as the men chanted, *"Hi-ya!"* over and over, lulling the others into a trance.

Arrow Keeper would bless each warrior's bonnet and shield so the white man's bullets could not find them. A Cheyenne who had painted and danced for war would face any danger, even sure death, with courage. But most braves would flee from a fight if their faces were ungreased and their bonnets not blessed.

With the brave named River of Winds attending him, Arrow Keeper took his place beside the same stump upon which Black Elk had stood earlier to speak to the tribe. He spotted Touch the Sky, dressed in new beaded buckskins, standing by himself and watching Honey Eater. With dread heavy in his belly, the old medicine man also noticed Black Elk watching both of them.

For a moment, Arrow Keeper wondered why Wolf Who Hunts Smiling was hanging back from the main circle and moving stiffly. Then the hot-blooded young Cheyenne turned just right in the light. Arrow Keeper winced when he saw that the youth's chest had been wrapped in soft bark dressings. The hateful stare he aimed at Touch the Sky left no doubt who had caused his wound.

"Warriors!" Arrow Keeper shouted. "Bring your gifts to the arrows!"

He unwrapped the pouch that contained the four sacred Medicine Arrows. Then he lay them carefully on the stump. Arrow Keeper prayed in a singsong chant to the Great Spirit while the males took turns filing by and making an offering to the arrows.

Death Chant

Black Elk left a pair of new chamois leggings.

River of Winds gave an elkskin wallet.

Swift Canoe knelt to leave a bone-handled knife.

Little Horse gave his only blanket.

High Forehead left a pair of quilled moccasins.

Touch the Sky sacrificed his only scalp, the hair he had lifted from the white man who had tried to kill him near Bighorn Falls.

Other warriors and warriors-in-training left twists of tobacco, buffalo robes, and pelts. Walking stiffly, his face wincing with pain, Wolf Who Hunts Smiling was the last to make an offering. He left a dressed deerskin.

As soon as Wolf Who Hunts Smiling had filed past, Arrow Keeper knelt to gather up the arrows. He reached one gnarled hand forward, then suddenly felt his breath hitch in his chest.

Too late, he realized he should not have let the wounded Wolf Who Hunts Smiling come close to the arrows. This was a terrible omen.

Fear making his scalp sweat, Arrow Keeper stared at the single scarlet drop of blood staining one of the arrows.

Chapter 7

Soon after he had announced his battle plan to the tribe, Black Elk divided the warriors into teams. Thus they could track and harass the scar-faced white and his bands of murdering thieves scattered throughout Cheyenne country.

Black Elk chose to lead his original group of warriors-in-training: his cousin Wolf Who Hunts Smiling, Swift Canoe, High Forehead, Little Horse, and Touch the Sky. Though he revealed little of his inner feelings, he was proud of his band's development as warriors.

From the scouts' initial reports, he knew that one band was marauding in the Powder River Valley near Yellow Bear's old summer camp. Their number was twice that of Black Elk's group, and they were well armed with new rifles. He was not sure where the scar-faced leader himself was. According to the scouts, this one often traveled from band to band, as if deliberately making it difficult to pin down his location.

One-half sleep after they had ridden out from the Tongue River camp, Black Elk stopped his band in a deep coulee near the Powder.

"Hear my words!" he said, addressing them from horseback. "Do not forget the talking paper at the trading post. Our enemies are not only the dogs we hunt down now. Every Cheyenne is a target for any paleface who wishes to kill red men for gold. Avoid riding along ridges, and do not ride away from the group alone."

His words sobered Touch the Sky and the others. The life of every red man had been endangered ever since the Bluecoats had invaded Indian territory. But now they were hunted like the buffalo, and like the buffalo their numbers were dwindling.

As if reading their thoughts, Black Elk added, "Remember the grief of your brother Walking Coyote when he found Buffalo Hump dead and scalped on the trail. Recall the wails and cries of the children and squaws when our dead braves were brought back to camp. *Shaiyena* blood has been shed and must be avenged. Our braves did not die the glorious death with the death song on their lips. They were cut down like dogs and now wander alone in the Forest of Tears!"

He raised his lance high. All six Cheyenne shouted, *"Hi-ya!"*

Touch the Sky felt his blood humming at Black Elk's words. Again he recalled Walking Coyote's grief as he had slashed his arms open over his dead brother. He had also made good on his vow to burn down his tipi and give away his horses. But by silent agreement, not one Cheyenne in camp dared mark them as his own. They would be fed and cared for until some tactful way could be found of giving them back to Walking Coyote. And though the mourning brave now slept alone at the edge of camp, he was under constant watch. Food was left for him in the night, and he would be stopped should he prepare to fall on his knife.

Despite their common cause as warriors, Touch the Sky was aware of great danger to him within the band. Since he had cut Wolf Who Hunts Smiling on the night of the Medicine Arrows ceremony, the younger Cheyenne was clearly bent on revenge. Ominously, Wolf Who Hunts Smiling no longer bothered to taunt him as before. But he watched Touch the Sky constantly. His wily, furtive stare never left the tall youth. His wolf eyes missed nothing.

Sensing this trouble before they left camp, Touch the Sky had chosen to ride his spirited dun instead of the handsome gray he had stolen from the Crow hunters. He had bested Wolf Who Hunts Smiling in a fight and saw no reason to antagonize him.

"What is the meaning of this?" Black Elk said in a demanding tone when they stopped later to water their horses in the river. He pointed toward the medicine bundle that Arrow Keeper had tied on the dun's bridle before Touch the Sky rode to the trading post. "Do you pretend to be a shaman?"

"Arrow Keeper tied it there," Touch the Sky said. The old medicine man had also tied a polished antelope horn filled with magic herbs around the pony's neck.

"Why did he do these things?"

"He told me it would make my horse faster and stronger," said Touch the Sky.

Scorn briefly touched Black Elk's stony features. The dead flap of his sewn-on ear looked like wrinkled rawhide in the glaring sunlight.

"So that is why you counted coup on the gray before my cousin could," he said. "Arrow Keeper shed the blood of many enemies in his youth. Now his medicine is strong. Since he placed these totems on your pony, I will leave them there. But put these words in your sash. No medicine will be strong enough to win Honey Eater from me. Do you understand this?"

Touch the Sky met the warrior's dark-eyed stare and refused to look away. "I hear the words you are saying to me," he finally answered.

"But you do not believe them?"

Touch the Sky continued to match his leader's stare. But this time he said nothing.

"Clearly," Black Elk said, his tone mocking, "the calf thinks he is a bull. Let us see, then, if he can lead the herd."

With Black Elk leading until that point, they had been tracking the whites along the Powder toward its confluence with the Yellowstone. They were well north of the Black Hills, the sacred center of the Cheyenne universe, and drawing dangerously close to the soldiertown called Fort Union. Without another word, Black Elk ordered Touch the Sky forward to ride as scout.

Wolf Who Hunts Smiling exchanged a knowing glance with Swift Canoe. Now they would exact some revenge for the beating Touch the Sky had recently given them!

At first, as he rode forward to the point position, Touch the Sky felt dread heavy in his belly. But he had paid close attention to Black Elk's repeated lessons in the art of tracking, and he recalled the things he had been taught. Soon he was absorbed in searching for the white murderers' trail.

In the beginning things went smoothly. The whites were traveling with many horses and heavily laden pack mules, and tracks were plentiful. But as his shadow began to lengthen in the westering sun, Touch the Sky abruptly encountered a great difficulty: the entire trail had been wiped out by a herd of wild horses. Further complicating matters, the whites had drifted far away from the river. Touch the Sky could not merely keep following the water and hope to pick the trail back up.

Black Elk rode behind the others and offered no advice. Wolf Who Hunts Smiling and Swift Canoe exchanged more glances, their eyes mocking Touch the Sky. After he had ridden in a wide circle, looking for sign, Touch the Sky recalled something he had once seen Black Elk do. He rode straight toward a tall cottonwood tree and quickly climbed up into the top branches.

The vast brown plain and the greener tableland of the river lay clear before him. The Powder, sluggish without the spring runoff to swell its banks, twisted and coiled northeast toward the point where it joined the Marias River at Fort Union. The fort was still well beyond the horizon. But Touch the Sky could see enough of the intervening landscape to make a good guess about their enemy's probable route. A series of deep cutbanks near the river explained why they had swerved wide. Yet they could not wander too far west from the river because the grass this far north was stunted and brown with the coming of the cold moons.

Touch the Sky made a map inside his head of the most likely route, memorizing a few features as landmarks. Then he climbed down again and, showing no hesitation in his face, led the others forward.

At first the tracks eluded him, and his heart began to sink. Then, just as Black Elk began to ride impatiently forward, he spotted a line of prints. Hope surging within his breast, Touch the Sky swung down off his pony to examine the prints. As Black Elk had taught them, he read the bend of the grass to determine how fresh they were. But the short grass made this difficult. He had better luck when he studied the mud inside the prints to see how much it had settled. They were no more than a few days old. The depth of many of them attested to the weight of heavily laden pack animals.

He rose again and gave his report to Black Elk. The war chief listened in impassive silence. But when Touch the Sky had finished, he nodded and said, "You have done well. Lead on."

Wolf Who Hunts Smiling's face was a malevolent mask of hatred. But for a moment, as Touch the Sky leaped up onto his pony, he thought he saw Little Horse watching him with a look of admiration. But the young Cheyenne quickly averted his eyes and pretended to be in conversation with High Forehead.

Again the trail was easy to follow. They rode in silence until the sun was only inches above the western horizon and the air was growing cool. The trail had passed the cutbanks and veered toward the river again. As they rounded a dogleg turn in the Powder, Touch the Sky immediately spotted signs of a huge camp.

Black Elk ordered them to dismount while he examined the signs all about them. The camp was recent. Embers dug out of the pile where a huge fire had been built were still warm to the touch. The white men had camped there at least one full sleep, judging from the quantity of human droppings just past the camp circle.

"Bad medicine remains wherever these murdering dogs have camped," said Black Elk. "We will ride well beyond this spot and make our own camp."

Black Elk selected a copse in a good patch of graze near the river. They tethered their ponies with rawhide strips, then spread their buffalo robes for the night. To be safe Black Elk decided on a cold camp. Their enemies were probably too sure of themselves—and perhaps too drunk—to bother posting sentries or sending anyone to double-check their back trail. But he did not want to risk a fire when he was not sure of the whites' location.

His band contented themselves with pemmican, dried plums, and cold river water. Touch the Sky had spread his robe well away from the others. But as he lay down and wrapped himself against the biting chill of the night air, he thought he could hear conspiring whispers from the direction of Wolf Who Hunts Smiling and Swift Canoe's robes.

A cool sweat broke out on his forehead. Black Elk had assured him that he did not value his life less than that of the others, that he would treat him fairly. But could the warrior truly feel that way after Honey Eater had returned his bride-price—and after Black Elk had seen her leaving Touch the Sky's tipi on the very same day of the rejection? What if Black Elk had merely said these things because he and Wolf Who Hunts Smiling were plotting to kill him and blame it on the white devils?

As the others began to fall asleep to the backdrop of the river's gentle purl, Touch the Sky imagined noises: rustling sounds, the snap of small twigs, the crush of leaves under moccasins.

Recalling Wolf Who Hunts Smiling's malevolent stares, he was unable to sleep. Finally he recalled a trick he had learned from the wily Pawnee leader War Thunder—the same trick that had saved the Pawnee's scalp when Wolf Who Hunts Smiling was about to lift it.

Moving as silently as he could, guiding himself by the light of a full moon, Touch the Sky gathered dead limbs and dried-up thorn bushes. With these he made a ring around his robe. Anyone trying to sneak up on him in the night would have to make noise.

The last thing he did before lying down again was lay his knife and Navy Colt handy in case they should be needed quickly. Somewhat reassured, he finally fell into an uneasy sleep.

"You got somethin' for us, Harlan?"

The bald, clean-shaven clerk named Harlan Perry looked up from the broad deal counter. Two bearded, long-haired men in buckskins were grinning at him. He recognized the one with the coarse-grained face as Jed Longstreet. The other was Stone McMasters. Both men worked for Henri Lagace, and Perry rued the day they had ever set foot into the Montana Territory.

Perry shot a nervous glance toward the small Lakota Sioux woman who was stacking pelts at the far end of the counter. He wished he had heard the men ride up so he could have sent his wife into the back room.

"I don't believe anything came in today, gentlemen," he said finally.

Longstreet dug a playful elbow into McMasters' ribs. "Aw, he's jist playin' the larks with us, ain'tcha, Harlan?"

When Perry said nothing, McMasters said, "You got a cob up your sitter? You know what we come for. Now git it."

"Gentlemen, no flatboat arrived today, so—"

"In a pig's ass!" Longstreet snarled, his pockmarked face twisted in drunken impatience. "Lagace ordered that alcohol weeks ago. Now you look real good and see if you got it."

Hearing their voices turn ugly, the Lakota woman, Sun Dance, had quietly rounded the counter. But before she could slip past the two foul-smelling whites, the one named McMasters reached out and roughly grabbed her by one arm.

"I ain't never planted my carrot in no red cow, Jed," he said to his companion. "I wunner how that feels?"

The moment McMasters grabbed his wife, Perry reached toward the scattergun he kept under the counter. But in the blink of an eye Longstreet lifted his big percussion-action Sharps rifle and planted the muzzle in the squaw's belly.

"If you're feelin' froggy, Harlan," he said in a low, dangerous voice, "you jist jump."

Perry dropped his hands to his side, knowing he was whipped. It had been a mistake to ever come out West, he realized again. Things had hummed along just fine until Henri Lagace and his hard-bitten followers had moved in. Now all the wanton killing, the distilling of powerful liquor to deliberately weaken the Indians and make them dependent—it was stirring up the white community to a frenzy. Soon it wouldn't be safe for a white man married to an Indian. He'd have to sell out and head back East.

"Wait a minutely, gentlemen," he said in a defeated voice. "Let me check again."

He rummaged under the counter. A moment later he wrestled a hefty wooden keg down on the counter in front of him.

"Well, wood ticks in my johnny!" Longstreet said. "Lookahere!"

Sun Dance finally struggled free of McMasters's grip and scurried into the back room. Watching the clerk with a mocking grin, Longstreet reached out and hugged the shipment of alcohol in one brawny arm. Lagace would be in a good mood when they arrived back at camp with this. It was time to boil up a new batch of Indian whiskey.

They were halfway to the door, hobnailed boots echoing on the raw puncheon floor, when Longstreet turned back around to stare at the dejected clerk. His coarse-grained face half in shadow under the broad brim of his plainsman's hat, Longstreet said, "You jist forget about them Injun-lovin' lubbers back East helpin' you out, Harlan. The only gum'ment out here is Henri Lagace and his gal Patsy."

To make his point clear, Longstreet raised the big Sharps again. "Harlan, meet Patsy Plumb!"

Chapter 8

While Black Elk's band was drawing nearer to the white marauders at the confluence of the Yellowstone and the Powder, Henri Lagace was traveling with the group he had sent to the Little Bighorn River valley.

This was well to the southwest of Black Elk's cold camp, between Sioux and Shoshone country. It was land where open plains alternated with vast mesquite flats and buttes. Lagace preferred this kind of territory because it made surprise Indian attacks on his well-armed packtrains much more unlikely.

Now, as the midmorning sun began to burn with its first real heat of the day, the steely-eyed Frenchman led his men in a southerly course paralleling the Little Bighorn. The packtrain moved slowly but steadily, many of the men leading pack animals by ropes secured to their saddle horns with half hitches. Jagged mountain spires rose majestically

76

into the sky on their right. The wide, empty plain stretched off to the horizon on their left. The sky was a vast, deep, bottomless blue spotted here and there by a thin white puff of cloud.

Even sitting his saddle, Lagace was obviously a tall man. He was thickset without running to fat, his long, yellow hair tied in a knot under the brim of his hat. Like the rest of his men, he wore fringed buckskins, the strings stiff and black with old blood. But the trait to which every eye was instantly drawn was the deep and raw gash that extended from the corner of his left eye well past the corner of his mouth.

Lagace never talked about that scar, and no one who knew him was foolish enough to ever mention it. He was a vain man who had once considered himself a favorite with the ladies. A Cheyenne tomahawk had ended all that.

He had received the scar six years earlier during the last mountain man rendezvous held on the Green River. In those days he had been a licensed trapper for the Northwest Company. One night he managed to trade a few bottles of whiskey for a huge cache of beaver pelts that a group of Cheyenne braves had brought to the rendezvous. While the Cheyenne were cavorting drunkenly, Lagace entered one of their tipis to rape the Indian's unmarried sister.

He made the mistake of picking a girl who was promised to one of the warriors. Even so, he might have gotten away with it if she had been Mandan or Crow. But he did not learn until it was too late that the Cheyenne valued chastity more than any other Plains Indians. Even alcohol couldn't blunt the warrior's wrath when he and the brother returned and discovered Lagace forcing himself on the girl.

Luckily for Lagace, another mountain man shot the buck before he could tug his tomahawk back out of the

Frenchman's face and deliver the deathblow. But to this day, though he hated all Indians, Lagace carried on a special vendetta against the Cheyenne.

"Keep your eyes skinned," he said now to Longstreet and McMasters, who rode beside him at the head of the packtrain. "We're entering Snake country."

Snake was the mountain man name for the Shoshone tribe. Lagace felt no real fear of attack from them. They were among the most poorly armed of the Plains Indians and notoriously bad shots with a rifle. His plan was to establish contact with a Snake chief and make his tribe a handsome gift of many bottles of liquor.

Longstreet backhanded the sweat off his coarse-grained face. "Hell's bells! I'm plumb sick of raggedy-ass redskins. I can't remember what it's like to rut on a white woman."

"Damn good thing you kin cook," McMasters said, "cuz with that face a yourn, you're lucky red wimmin'll let you poke 'em."

Almost immediately he realized what he had said. The eyes Lagace turned on him were as cold and dead and flat as two stones. McMasters clamped his mouth shut and stared off toward the mountains.

They crested a long rise and Lagace halted the packtrain. He was riding a handsome sorrel gelding he had acquired in a trade with a cavalry officer. It was the fastest animal he had ever encountered on the plains, faster even than the best Indian ponies. His sorrel had never been outrun and had never lost a race.

He leaned back against the cantle of his handsome, hand-tooled saddle. He broke out a pair of U.S. Army field glasses. Carefully, patiently, he scanned the entire area before him, looking for any sign of Indians.

Lagace had earned a good living as a legitimately licensed trapper. But ironically, the fate of the rugged mountain men depended directly on the state of fashion in dandified London: as beaver-pelt hats began to go out of fashion, the price of plews, or beaver furs, began to drop. With too many fur-trading companies already working the best beaver streams, this drop in prices began to squeeze out the free trappers. Many of them ended up marooned in the frontier, bitter and disgruntled.

There was still a market for plews, but the low prices did not justify the hard work of trapping or the constant struggle for survival. Lagace had already learned there was an easier way to make quick profits: robbing the traps of others. It was a stroke of genius when he came up with the idea of not only blaming his enemy the Cheyenne, but also profiting from Cheyenne scalps.

He recruited his own private army of frontier hardcases and cutthroats. This was easy, given the number of criminals and malcontents who had fled the law in the East. Once driven out of the trapping business by falling prices and organized companies, many were eager to serve a ruthless, cunning leader who would assure their survival in a harsh land.

By now he had organized a group that numbered almost 100 men, currently divided into four roving bands. Lagace was the linchpin, the key to holding these highly individual, often dangerous, personalities together. He ruled with an iron hand and doled out the only two things they would respond to: money and violence.

The territorial vigilantes welcomed their presence because they were a direct threat to the Indians. Drunk Indians occasionally committed atrocities against white settlers. But in general a drunk Indian was as easy to control as a child.

Occasionally the Army, in a halfhearted gesture to the politicians and reformers back East, threatened to disband Lagace's private army. But so far, generous bribes to the right colonels and generals had eliminated that threat. The biggest danger by far was the Indians themselves. However, they were always busy warring with each other and didn't have the common sense to organize for their own good. His liquor, which he always supplied free until the Indians were addicted and would do anything to get it, took care of the rest.

Still, Lagace was vaguely troubled as he carefully searched the vast plains. He had heard, through a Pawnee who served as a scout for the Seventh Cavalry, that a tribe of Cheyenne was on the warpath against him. Such news traveled fast through the Indian nations. Now he needed to capture some redskins and learn as many details as he could.

And suddenly, he discovered his opportunity.

He focused the field glasses for a better look. Below, perhaps a mile off across the plain, a trio of Indians stood near the edge of a stand of scrub oak. They had built a fire and were roasting a freshly killed elk. While the meat cooked, they were eating boiled guts. Using one hand to force the contents of the intestines down, they devoured the gut behind it.

"Snakes, all right," Lagace thought without bothering to study the Indians' features more closely. He knew the Shoshone considered boiled intestines a delicacy.

Lagace lifted one hand high, signaling the packtrain to stop and rest where they were. "Follow me," he said to Longstreet and McMasters. "But hold your mounts to a trot."

Rifle butts protruding from their saddle scabbards, the three white men descended the rise and pointed their bridles toward the Shoshone. Busy over their meal, the Indians did not notice the new arrivals until they were well on them. Lagace had pulled a white truce flag out of his saddlebag and held it high as they approached.

The Indians glanced toward their ponies, tethered nearby. But the palefaces would be upon them before they could mount and flee. Lagace watched them confer briefly among themselves. Apparently they decided to trust the flag. Their faces impassive, they watched the whites approach.

Lagace could speak a few words in several Indian tongues. He greeted the Shoshones in a crude mixture of their own and Crow languages, knowing the Crow were their allies in battle. "We are friends of the red man. We have gifts for your chief."

The oldest of the three braves was named Sioux Killer. He had once been a guide for mountain men and had learned English. He looked at his companions, Red Bull and Thunderhead. Barely moving his head, Red Bull signaled his distrust.

"We have gifts," Lagace repeated in his mixture of Shoshone and Crow. "We want to parley."

Lagace said something to Longstreet, and the cook pulled a necklace of brightly colored baubles and trinkets out of his saddlebag. It caught the sun's rays and glowed in a rainbow of pretty colors. All three Shoshone stared, captivated.

"We want to parley," Lagace repeated.

Sioux Killer glanced back up at the scar-faced white. "What do you wish from us?" he said in thick but understandable English.

Lagace resisted a smile as he realized his luck— an English-speaking informant! He dismounted and told his companions to do likewise. He took the necklace from Longstreet and carried it over to Sioux Killer.

"Our business concerns your enemies, the Cheyenne. We have heard of a plan. One of the Cheyenne chiefs is on the warpath against me. The enemy of your people is the enemy of my people. Who is this Cheyenne chief, and where are his clan circles camped?"

Sioux Killer again glanced at his companions. It was true the Shoshone were allies of the Crow and enemies of the Cheyenne and Sioux. However, they were not presently at war with either tribe. Of course Sioux Killer had heard of the plan this scar-face spoke of. Yellow Bear had sent word-bringers throughout the plains, asking his allies the Sioux and the Arapahoe to join the fight. The Shoshone had learned this much through spies.

However, Sioux Killer also knew that all red men had a dangerous common enemy in the whites. The necklace glittered in his fingers. Speaking in his own tongue, he explained to his companions what it was the white man wanted.

"Brothers, this thing would be left alone," Red Bull advised. "I have no love for the bloodthirsty Cheyenne who killed my father. How many times have they stolen our horses and stolen our meat? But these palefaces, they are bad medicine."

"Truly they are," Thunderhead agreed. "But may we not wear the mask of friendship and acquire more of these fine gifts? These are only long knives. Speak in a wolf bark, but put on the face of a friend. They have stolen from the red man, let us now steal from them."

Sioux Killer considered this and decided he liked it. He gestured toward the fire, offering the three white men some meat. "Eat!"

Longstreet spat into the dirt. Then he removed a plug of tobacco from his possibles bag and gnawed off a hunk. "These Injuns don't know shit from apple butter," he said impatiently. "I say we jist put 'em under."

"Shut up," Lagace said, fixing his steely-eyed stare on the cook. "I want your opinion, I'll beat it out of you."

Lagace returned to his gelding and removed a bottle of whiskey from the saddlebags. It was from a fresh batch of his notorious Indian whiskey brewed from straight alcohol boiled with river water, gunpowder, and chewing tobacco. He pulled the cork out with his teeth and carried the bottle over to Sioux Killer, handing it to him. He repeated his question about the Cheyenne.

Sioux Killer, who remembered the joys of drunkenness from his days with the mountain men, accepted it eagerly. But as he drank and passed the bottle to his companions, he played dumb. His face was friendly, but it was as if his English had somehow been lost.

"They figger they got us buffaloed," McMasters said. But he remembered Lagace's warning to Longstreet, and he said nothing else.

Lagace was more patient. He knew it wouldn't take long for the powerful liquor to oil the Indians' tongues. Again he repeated his question, throwing in as many Shoshone and Crow phrases as he could remember. Again Sioux Killer feigned friendliness, but shook his head as if he didn't understand.

At first the plan to loosen his tongue with alcohol backfired. As the Indians began to get crazy drunk, they started to mock the whites among themselves in their own tongue.

"Brothers!" Red Bull said. "Are these hairy-faced dogs all blind? Do you see how they stick their stinking faces right up to ours when they speak? And they shout as if we were on the far side of a vast canyon."

"Yes, this is surely true, brother," Thunderhead agreed. "And have you smelled of them good? Phew! I have smelled carrion, many moons gone with maggots, that does not reek as they do!"

"I have smelled this stink indeed," Red Bull said. "And jabber? They are like chattering chipmunks, wasting words as if they have no importance. Palefaces speak merely to hear themselves make noise, and thus they cheapen the importance of talk."

Longstreet pawed at his coarse-grained face, clearly impatient. Even Lagace was showing signs of short temper. But in their drunkenness the Shoshone failed to see these signs.

"Look there, brothers!" Red Bull said, pointing at Lagace's fancy calfskin boots. "How can they walk or ride or sneak up on their enemies when they wrap their feet in hides as stiff as the Bluecoat saddles?"

This struck all three Indians as hilarious. Unable to control themselves, they rolled on the ground shaking with gales of mirth.

Cursing, Lagace said something to his two companions. They walked to their saddles and returned with their rifles. Lagace drew his .32-caliber Colt Patterson pistol out of his sash. While he covered the surprised Indians, Longstreet and McMasters tied Red Bull down spread-eagle near the fire.

Lagace repeated his question to Sioux Killer about the location of the Cheyenne camp. Still the brave feigned incomprehension.

Longstreet kicked Red Bull in the ribs. "Cut off his pizzle. They'll palaver then, by beaver!"

Calmly, Lagace grabbed a burning limb out of the fire and shoved the glowing end into Red Bull's exposed stomach. His scream hurt the ears of his companions. The stench of scorched flesh wafted to their nostrils.

Shock and anger glazed Sioux Killer and Thunderhead's eyes.

"They look mad enough to grease hell with war paint!" McMasters said gleefully, digging at a tick in his beard. "Wouldn't they love to raise our hair!"

This time, when Lagace repeated his question, Sioux Killer responded in English. He named the Cheyenne chief Yellow Bear and gave the exact location of his camp on the Tongue River.

"Hell's bells!" said Longstreet. "That-air's the tribe that young buck at the trading post mentioned!"

Sioux Killer had remained on the ground during all this. Now Lagace squatted on his rowels and made the Shoshone swear on his medicine bundle that he had spoken the straight word. Then he stood back up and nodded to his men.

Without a word Longstreet drew his knife from its sheath. He bent down over Red Bull and made a deep slash in his lower belly, gutting him. He was an expert at this. The Indian's intestines spilled out before his own terrified eyes, yet he didn't die instantly.

"Brothers!" Red Bull cried out. "They have cut me open like a buffalo!"

He tried to sing the Shoshone death song, but the shock and pain set in before he could utter the words. The last sound from his throat was the death rattle.

Tears brimming in their eyes at the fate of their red brother, Sioux Killer and Thunderhead started to sing the death song. McMasters and Lagace fired almost simultaneously, shooting both of them in the brain.

Longstreet chuckled, staring at the coiled white guts spilling out of the dead Red Bull. "There! Le'me see him stick anything in his meatbag now!"

Judd Cole

Lagace returned to his mount and stepped up into leather. He was content. He had learned the name of his enemies and the location of their village. It was time to take the bull by the horns and to strike first.

Chapter 9

For two more sleeps Black Elk's band tracked the whites along the twisting route of the Powder River. They were in the northern reaches of Sioux country, skirting the Crow nation to the west and approaching the hunting grounds of the northern tribe known as the Assiniboin. Although they encountered no Indians along the trail, there were clear signs that the white men had: twice the Cheyenne found spots where unshod Indian ponies had mingled with the shod horses and mules of the packtrain. These were clearly friendly meetings, judging from the number of empty liquor bottles littering the area.

Worse, when the Indians ponies had left, at least one made far deeper prints than the others—suggesting, Black Elk pointed out grimly, that the red visitors had taken a plentiful supply of devil water back to the tribe with them.

"Clearly," he said to his band, "the palefaces are spreading their poison throughout the Indian nations. Now they call the strong water a gift and assure us there will be more. But soon it will not be a gift. The red man will give everything—his hides, his horses, his meat, his women even—to obtain more. In his drunken sloth he will forget the pride and skills of the warrior. And soon, like the once-proud peoples east of the Great Waters, he will be herded onto reservations. He will stop hunting and grow corn, he will answer the Bluecoat's roll call, and he will beg like a dog for any scraps the white man might toss to him!"

They were still one-half sleep below the confluence of the Powder and the Yellowstone when they discovered horse droppings still fresh enough to be moist.

"Ride out ahead," Black Elk said to his cousin Wolf Who Hunts Smiling. "Use the arts of concealment I have taught you. Sneak up as close as you can to our enemy and study them well. If they are in camp when you find them, learn where they position their guards. Make a picture in your mind and bring it back to me."

Wolf Who Hunts Smiling held his face impassive and only nodded. But Touch the Sky and the others knew he was swollen with pride at the importance of this mission. He had been chafing ever since Black Elk's approval of Touch the Sky's skill at reading sign. Here at last was a chance to prove his own superiority.

Toward the middle of the afternoon, when their shadows were starting to lengthen in the sun, Wolf Who Hunts Smiling came galloping back to join them.

"Cousin!" he greeted Black Elk excitedly. "Our enemies have reached the place where the two rivers join, and clearly they plan to remain there for some time. They are erecting a rope corral for their animals and unpacking all of their equipment."

"It is as I feared," Black Elk said. "This spot is in the midst of the Indian nations. From there they can easily send word to the Sioux, the Crow, the Blackfeet, the Assiniboin, the Mandan, the Hidatsa. Is the scar-face with them?"

Wolf Who Hunts Smiling shook his head. "Nor the two hairy faces we saw enter the trading post, the two who always accompany him."

Black Elk's disappointment was keen. He already knew from the initial report of the scouts Yellow Bear had sent out that the scar-faced leader traveled from band to band. Nonetheless, Black Elk had hoped to surprise and kill him.

Black Elk glanced overhead to judge how much daylight remained. Then he made up his mind. "Now we must ride hard and strike quickly. We cannot attack the main body. But we will set up a lure. A herd divided weakens itself. Just as a good hunter always isolates a buffalo for the kill, we must draw a few white dogs from the protection of the pack!"

Before they rode on, he explained his strategy. He wanted the whites to know that they were being watched and followed, that death might strike any one of them at any moment. Black Elk spoke of Bluecoats who had gone *Wendigo*, insane, from this type of pressure, who had fled alone into the wilderness to meet sure death rather than live in death's shadow.

Black Elk's plan for their first strike was simple. First the Cheyenne would find a good hiding place for the main body of their band. Then Black Elk, riding alone, would appear to accidentally ride in sight of the camp. Since the whites were apparently killing every Cheyenne they encountered, they would surely send some riders after him.

If there were too many, he would lose them and return to the hiding place.

"But if the number is small enough," he concluded, "I will lead them to your position. It will be up to you to kill them. Show me that you are true braves, and I will lead our entire village in honoring you when you hang our enemies' scalps from our lodgepoles!"

Touch the Sky felt a tightening in his chest as the band neared the white men's camp, Wolf Who Hunts Smiling leading now. They stuck to the scrub oaks at the rim of the river valley. They crested a long line of hills and suddenly the confluence of the Powder and the Yellowstone was visible below on their right.

So, too, was their enemy's camp. It was just as Wolf Who Hunts Smiling had described it. White men bustled about everywhere, unpacking crates and panniers. The rope corral was completed and the horses and mules herded into it. Everywhere they went, the men made sure to carry their rifles.

"They have posted no guards yet," Black Elk said. "But they will before nightfall. We will have a surprise for them after darkness settles, too. But now, ride quietly and follow me."

They veered due west away from the camp. The terrain there was mostly hills alternating with sandstone shoulders. They rode until they found a narrow defile that led between two hills. Black Elk led them around behind one of the hills, then up to its summit. He positioned his band behind a cluster of boulders.

"Remember," he said, "if too many follow me, I will be returning alone. If not, you must be ready. I will try to slow them below you, but your shots must count. One bullet, one enemy! One arrow, one enemy!"

Only Touch the Sky and Wolf Who Hunts Smiling, who still had the Colt rifle that had once belonged to Touch the Sky, had firearms. Little Horse owned a scattergun, which he had captured from the white miner he killed in Bighorn Falls. But it was back at Yellow Bear's camp, useless until he could obtain more shells. Like Swift Canoe and High Forehead, he was armed with a buffalo-sinew bow and a stone-tipped lance.

After issuing his final instructions, Black Elk rode back alone in the direction of the white men's camp. As he waited behind a boulder, Touch the Sky could not help admiring Black Elk's courage in spite of the fact that the warrior hated him. It was a dangerous thing, purposely showing himself to such treacherous men—men who were taking Cheyenne scalps and selling them for gold.

But as he waited, impatience knotting inside his stomach like a tight fist, Black Elk's words drifted back to him: "There must come a time when Honey Eater either accepts my horses or you and I must fight to the death."

Again Touch the Sky felt his fear of several nights earlier returning. Though he was still not a blooded warrior like Black Elk, he had at least counted coup on their Crow enemies—and Black Elk himself had seen it. This was not an impressive record for a buck with dreams of marrying a chief's daughter, but it was at least a start. So, too, was the handsome gray horse he had stolen from the Crow. Touch the Sky had decided not to ride it. Instead, it would be saved as the beginning of the bride-price for Honey Eater.

But would he live to offer the bride-price? Touch the Sky glanced to his left, where Wolf Who Hunts Smiling and Swift Canoe were huddled together. Had Black Elk meant the thing he promised about treating him fairly? Or was that merely intended to throw off his suspicions so that the others could more easily kill him? Touch the Sky knew that a war leader—like a peace chief—was above tribal law. For this very reason, any leader was expected to always be just and fair. But being above the law also left Black Elk incredible power to do evil without answering for it. What would a brave do for love of Honey Eater?

Suddenly his thoughts scattered like chaff in the wind as pounding hoofbeats reached them.

"Here comes Black Elk!" said Little Horse, who was huddled on Touch the Sky's right with High Forehead. Little Horse held his bow with an arrow notched. "Now be ready! Two whites are following close on his heels!"

A rifle shot rang out below, another. They heard Black Elk shout a taunting "*Hi-ya!*" to his pursuers. More quickly than they expected, the three riders entered the narrow defile below them.

Wolf Who Hunts Smiling was determined to make the first kill. He flopped on his stomach over the boulder, drawing a bead on the first white. A moment later he squeezed his trigger and there was a flat, metallic click. His rifle had misfired.

Touch the Sky, busy aiming his pistol, was only vaguely aware of this. He was about to shoot when, suddenly, he was knocked to the ground by a flying weight. It took him a moment to understand: Wolf Who Hunts Smiling had jumped him to keep him from making the kill!

While the two struggled in the dirt behind the boulders, Little Horse let fly his arrow. It pierced the first white clean through the neck and dropped him from his saddle. Swift Canoe and High Forehead loosed their arrows at the second rider. One struck him in the upper left arm, the other in the back. When he turned his horse to flee, Black Elk whirled around and shot him from his saddle.

Meantime, the two young Cheyenne struggled in the dirt. Touch the Sky had the size and weight advantage, but Wolf Who Hunts Smiling had stunned him when he slammed into him. They gripped for each other's throats and gouged eyes, each trying to heave the other loose and leap on him.

Suddenly Touch the Sky felt an iron grip tearing him loose from his adversary. Black Elk stood over them, his normally passive face twisted in open scorn.

"Two Cheyenne warriors!" he said, his voice heavy with disgust. "Clawing each other in the dirt like women while their enemy escapes them! Do you realize this thing you have done? For myself, I do not value my life more than a gnat's. But do you realize the seriousness of letting a war chief be killed? My obligation is to my people. You did not merely endanger me—you endangered your entire tribe!"

Overcome with contempt, he turned to the others. "You braves! And from this day I call you braves! Quickly, go below and take the scalps you have earned. But quickly, for soon the palefaces will send many riders out to see what delays these two."

As he sat up, blood running from a gash in his cheek, Touch the Sky felt himself swelling with rage and shame. Had the others not seen that Wolf Who Hunts Smiling had jumped him first? But when he glanced at Little Horse and High Forehead, they were already scuttling below to carry out Black Elk's orders.

Black Elk aimed a final glance at Wolf Who Hunts Smiling and Touch the Sky. "An Indian who does not place his tribe before his own pride is useless as a warrior. Only through the tribe do we live on. I consider both of you no better than enemies until you prove that I am wrong."

"But cousin," Wolf Who Hunts Smiling protested, "it was not I who—"

"Silence!" Black Elk said, cutting him off. "I have no ears to hear your words. A warrior's worth is measured in deeds, not words. I repeat, from this time forth, until you prove otherwise, I consider both of you no better than enemies of Yellow Bear's tribe!"

Chapter 10

Honey Eater rose before her father and dressed quickly in the chill morning air. Then she raised the flap over the entrance to their tipi and stood in the opening for a few minutes, gazing out over the camp and thinking. The night before she had picked fresh white columbine and left it pressed between wet leaves. Now she carefully braided her hair with it.

Down toward the river, mist still hovered in ghostly pockets. It would not burn off until the sun cleared the hills that sheltered the Tongue River Valley. Normally the camp would be quiet at this hour, though it often remained noisy and active far into the night. But with this terrible threat hanging over the Cheyenne, camp life had been disrupted. Gold for their scalps! How could human beings be reduced to nothing more than beaver pelts? Honey Eater found it difficult to hate anyone. But she hated the Pawnee with all her soul for killing her mother and bringing such bloodshed and misery to her people. And she hated the whites for placing a bounty on the Cheyenne.

With the warriors out tracking their white enemies, the old men, children, and women had taken over the defense of the camp. Sentries ringed the village day and night, and more worked in shifts within the camp itself. Everyone except the smallest children carried weapons with them everywhere. Anyone who attacked them would pay dearly for scalps.

Behind her, old Yellow Bear stirred in his robes, coming to life for the day. Hearing him reminded her of her obligations. She stepped outside and stirred the charred wood beneath the tripod. It had grown cold during the night. She walked to the nearest tipi where a fire was blazing and borrowed a piece of glowing punk. Then she returned to the tripod and started the morning fire.

For a moment she hesitated in her labors, glancing suspiciously out past the river. For a second she had felt a premonition of danger that made her blood run cold. But a moment later it passed.

Yellow Bear's meat rack stood behind the tipi. She selected two fresh elk steaks and dropped them, dripping with marrow fat, onto the tripod. Soon the meat was sizzling, the delicious odor wafting back into the tipi. The tantalizing smell was enough to wake Yellow Bear from his slumber.

"Good morning, little daughter," his gravelly voice said behind her.

She turned to greet him. The Cheyenne chief had wrapped his red Hudson's bay blanket around him, long silver locks spilling down over his shoulders. Lines radiated from his eyes like parched tributaries.

Honey Eater served him, then sat beside him to eat her own meal. When she had finished she went back inside the tipi to prepare for the morning's instruction at the women's lodge. There, older squaws taught the unmarried girls the domestic arts of tribal life. Most important was the elaborate beadwork and embroidery for which Cheyenne women were famous throughout the plains.

Honey Eater gathered up a robe she was decorating with quillwork embroidery. This, and a beaded shawl to be worn at her squaw-taking ceremony, would be part of the many valuable gifts she would present to her husband in exchange for the bride-price he paid her family.

This time, as she was leaving the tipi, Yellow Bear surprised her by placing his gnarled hand on her smooth brown arm to halt her. "Daughter, I would have a word with you."

She stopped and stood with her eyes cast respectfully down, in the way that younger Cheyenne listened when elders were speaking.

"Honey Eater," he said, his voice kind and patient, "have you considered well this thing with Black Elk?"

His words did not surprise her. Yellow Bear had been troubled ever since she prevailed upon him to send Black Elk's horses back.

"Yes, father, I have."

"Have your wishes changed?"

Honey Eater shook her head.

Yellow Bear sighed and gazed out over the camp. This thing was awkward. Any Cheyenne father, but particularly a chief, was expected to show more authority in the question of his daughter's marriage. But Honey Eater reminded him of his wife Singing Woman, who had been killed by Pawnee warriors before Honey Eater's eyes.

"Do you understand," he said, "what Black Elk has done for the tribe? How brave he is?"

"Yes. I admire Black Elk greatly. War has made him hard, but not mean."

Yellow Bear nodded at the wisdom of this remark. Truly this good girl was like her mother!

"Is there no way, daughter," he said, gently persisting, "that your heart may melt toward him?"

This time Honey Eater took a long time before answering. She could not openly admit yet to her father that her heart was already filled with love for Touch the Sky. Again, she thought about how magnificent he appeared to her: taller already than most adult braves, broad in the shoulders, his eyes keen and dark and handsome.

She knew that Black Elk was a strong, brave man, a blooded warrior. But thinking of him did not make her smile inside herself as she did when she thought about Touch the Sky. And though he, too, was a Cheyenne by birth, there was something different about Touch the Sky that excited her. That one memorable night when they had met secretly in the shadow of the council lodge, he had pressed his lips to her hair briefly, and her heart had raced as if she had run a great distance. She had never heard of red men doing such a thing, yet it thrilled her.

But he, too, was a brave warrior. For a moment Honey Eater almost forgot her promise to Arrow Keeper. She almost told her father how brave and magnificent Touch the Sky had been during the Pawnee attack when he saved Yellow Bear's life by killing the Pawnee leader, War Thunder. But only she and Arrow Keeper had witnessed his bravery.

Instead, she said simply, "Father, you know I will never disobey you. If you tell me I must marry Black Elk, I will. I will be a good wife to him. But my heart does not embrace him as a husband."

Yellow Bear's seamed face was troubled. In his heart he knew that Honey Eater loved Touch the Sky. He understood that the young buck was pleasing to look at, and he had made great progress in learning the Cheyenne way, considering his wretched ignorance when he joined the tribe. If Honey Eater were not the daughter of a chief, Yellow Bear would not be so troubled by her choice.

But she was the daughter of a chief, and there were other considerations. Every ten years, in the spring when the snows melted and game was again plentiful, there was a chief-renewal ceremony. Yellow Bear was in the final year of his chieftainship, and he was glad it was almost over. A medicine dream had already told him that he would not live to see the next greening of the grass. The last important thing to do before he crossed to the Land of Ghosts was to see Honey Eater settled in the right marriage. And Black Elk was clearly the right marriage.

True, Black Elk was too young yet to serve as a peace chief. He would certainly be passed up at the next chief-renewal. But he was already a war leader, and in ten more winters it would certainly be his time to lead the tribe. The others in the tribe expected this thing to pass.

"Hear my words, little daughter," he said, his voice taking on an edge of authority. "I will not use my power as your father—not yet. But know that just as a chief has influence over his people, they have influence over him. He is the voice of the tribe, but the collective wish of the people is the will. Do you understand this thing?"

Eyes still downcast, Honey Eater nodded.

"The time will come when you must accept Black Elk's horses. Now I have finished speaking. Take my words away with you and examine them carefully."

Her heart heavy with the sad truth of her father's words, Honey Eater crossed the camp toward the women's lodge at the far side. By now a large group of children had assembled in the middle of camp to play at their favorite game, going on the warpath. Honey Eater stopped for a few moments to watch them.

The children had divided into two camps, one pretending to be a hostile tribe. The boys played at fighting like seasoned braves, taking captives and counting coups. They tied bunches of buffalo hair to poles for scalps and carried lances made of willow branches. Their shields were bent willow shoots with the leafy twigs hanging down like feathers. They also carried little bows and arrows.

While the boys fought and charged, yipping the war cry, the girls stood ready to pull down the make-believe lodges built from branches. If the battle went badly against their group, they would gather the branches up and begin to run away.

Watching them play, Honey Eater felt sad. This was no game. How well the children had learned the lessons about life as a Cheyenne! Still carrying her robe and beaded shawl, she finished crossing to the women's lodge. Right before she entered, she stopped again and gazed out across the surrounding forests and hills.

Once again a chill of premonition passed through her like ice water in her veins. But surely, she told herself, if there were danger the sentries would sound the familiar wolf howl of alarm.

Her pretty face troubled and preoccupied, she raised the flap and entered the lodge.

From his vantage point on a ridge overlooking the Tongue River, Henri Lagace watched Yellow Bear's camp stir to life for the day.

His field glasses gave him a good view of the tipis in their neat clan circles. He knew that the chief's tipi always stood in the midst of camp, yet apart from the clans. So he also knew that the old man in the red blanket must be Yellow Bear, and the pretty girl with white columbine in her hair his daughter.

He watched her as she crossed the camp, carrying her robe and beaded shawl. The flawless beauty of her smooth, amber-tinted skin evoked his ire and the deep hatred he felt for the Cheyenne tribe. For a moment he raised one hand to feel the deep, ragged trench caused by the tomahawk scar that had ruined his face. How satisfying it would be, he thought, to likewise destroy the beauty of her unmarred face.

He watched her enter the hide-covered lodge. A plan was already forming in his mind. He had left the main body of his men, 25 strong and well armed, hidden back in the dense trees bordering the river well south of the camp. Lagace, assisted by McMasters and Longstreet, had already thoroughly scouted the area. They knew there were too many sentries for a surprise attack en masse.

Although there were few braves to defend them, Lagace knew that Cheyenne women and children could be fierce fighters when attacked in their own camp. He and his men might be able to kill old Yellow Bear, but it would be a costly attack.

It would be even better, Lagace thought, still watching the lodge the girl had just entered, to nab the chief's daughter. She could then be used indefinitely as ransom. Either Yellow Bear called off this war against him or the girl died. Eventually, she might even serve as a lure to seize Yellow Bear himself.

In time, of course, the girl, Yellow Bear, and all of the Cheyenne would be killed. To Lagace, Indians were nits, and as he often repeated to his men, nits made lice.

Only, in this case, he had cleverly arranged it so that those particular nits were worth gold. The immediate problem, as he knew from his scouts' reports, were those Cheyenne war parties presently out dogging him and his men. It was necessary to kidnap the girl and, thus, make the appearance of negotiating. Then the war parties would be called off.

Lagace imitated the sound of a thrush. In a few minutes he was joined by Longstreet and McMasters, who had been posted on either side of him.

"You," he said to the coarse-faced Longstreet, "go back and pick five men. Take them up to that long ridge over there on the south side of the camp. When I give the signal, open up with diversionary fire. Kill as many as you want to. But don't forget the locations of the sentries, and keep your eyes skinned for them. Be sure you slip past them unnoticed."

He turned to McMasters, who was busy digging at a tick in his beard. "You," he said, "are going down into the village with me. Every able-bodied redskin down there is going to rush to the south of camp, figuring it's an attack. We're going into that lodge and grabbing the chief's daughter."

"Into the lodge!" said McMasters. "Christ Jesus! They'll lift our topknots."

Lagace turned his dead, flat eyes on his lackey. "It's filled with unarmed women. You think you can face that?"

McMasters grinned, revealing teeth stained the color of licorice spit. "I reckon I kin, at that."

"There'll be no time for what you're thinking," said Lagace. "We're after the chief's daughter, that's all. We have to get in and out of there quick."

Longstreet left to carry the message to the main body. Lagace and McMasters moved carefully forward, avoiding the sentries as they positioned themselves closer for the strike. Nearly two hours passed while they impatiently slapped at flies and watched the sun climb higher in the sky. Finally Lagace spotted the signal he was waiting for: three quick flashes from the shard of mirror Longstreet carried in his possibles bag for just such occasions.

Lagace pulled his .31-caliber Colt-Patterson pistol from his sash and fired one shot into the air. Instantly, all hell was loosed at the far end of the Cheyenne camp. Hidden rifles opened fire, dropping children and old people as if they were fish in a barrel. Screams broke loose below. Just as Lagace had predicted, the entire camp rushed to defend against the attack.

Lagace and McMasters had already broken into a run down the side of the hill. The women's lodge was at the edge of camp closest to their position, and they were drawing near by the time the first girl, her face drained of blood in her fright, lifted the entrance flap and rushed outside.

Honey Eater was the second one to run outside. By now the two white men were close enough to be spotted. An old woman who came out behind Honey Eater drew a bone-handle knife from her dress. Longstreet lifted his big Sharps and blew a hole the size of a fist in her chest.

Seeing the old woman fall, her chest spuming blood, Honey Eater made the instinctive mistake of turning back to help the squaw. Lagace closed on her fast.

Her face defiant, she began singing the death song even as she clawed at the rawhide thong around her neck, pulling something out from under her buckskin dress.

Lagace knew the Cheyenne tribe well enough to know what she was doing. The thong in her hand held a small knife, which all young Cheyenne women wore in case of the threat of capture. They valued chastity so strongly that they would rather kill themselves than face the possibility of defilement by rape. The woman he had assaulted had tried to stab herself before he beat her senseless.

He reached her just as she was about to plunge the short, wide blade into her breast. He backhanded her in the temple with the muzzle of his pistol, and she collapsed unconscious.

McMasters, stained teeth showing through his red-streaked beard, was drawing a bead on the back of a fleeing girl.

"Never mind that, you jackass!" roared Lagace. He picked up the unconscious girl as easily as if she were a rag puppet. "Cover my back trail! Let's get the hell out of here before the rest figure out what's happening!"

Chapter 11

Unaware of the tragedy back at Yellow Bear's camp, Touch the Sky and the rest of Black Elk's band continued harassing their white enemies in the style of warfare the Cheyenne had learned from battles with the Apache. They attacked alone or in small groups, striking swiftly, silently, and without being seen.

For nearly three sleeps they continued their assault on the white men's nerves. A sentry was found with an arrow through his heart and his scalp missing. A sniper's bullet cut another man down as he was relieving himself in the river. But each time the angry enemy sent a well-armed party out to scour the surrounding hills and plains, no sign of Indians could be found.

"You have done well," Black Elk told his band on the third night following the ambush of the two white riders. "Now our enemies sleep with one eye open, jumping to their feet at the hoot of an owl or the scream of a wildcat."

They had made a cold camp in the shelter of a limestone outcropping well downriver from the enemy camp. A full moon reflected off the pale limestone, providing a soft glow like foxfire. Touch the Sky could just make out the features of the others in the dim light.

"Tonight," Black Elk said, "we will pluck the eagle while he is sleeping in his nest! One of us will sneak into their corral and scatter their horses and mules while another distracts the sentry."

Although his words were meant for all of them, Black Elk looked only at Little Horse, High Forehead, and Swift Canoe—the three he had called braves after the ambush. Still angry at Touch the Sky and Wolf Who Hunts Smiling for their behavior, he ignored them. When he was forced to speak to them, his manner was harsh and abrupt.

Black Elk's manner influenced the other three. Before the ambush, Little Horse and High Forehead had simply ignored Touch the Sky, pretending he did not exist. Since Touch the Sky had shamed himself by fighting with Wolf Who Hunts Smiling when his tribe needed him, the other youths had adopted Black Elk's tone, speaking to him with unhidden coldness and hostility. Even Swift Canoe had changed in his friendship with Wolf Who Hunts Smiling. Since being called a brave by Black Elk, Swift Canoe did not fawn over his old friend nor sit alone with him.

All of this only served to increase Wolf Who Hunts Smiling's hatred for Touch the Sky. He blamed his enemy for all of his troubles. But Touch the Sky's main concern was to somehow prove to the others—especially to Little Horse, whose friendship he sorely missed—that he did care deeply about the tribe.

Black Elk walked toward the river for a moment. When

he returned, he held six pieces of reed in his hand.

"Whoever draws the shortest reed," he said, "will also draw the dangerous duty of scattering the horses and mules. He who pulls the next shortest will distract the sentry. It will not be possible to kill him. There is too much open ground between the guard and the shelter of trees. It will be necessary to make a slight noise—enough to cause him to investigate, but not so much that he raises the cry of alarm.

"When the guard is distracted, our man must cross the open ground and use his knife to cut the rope corral. He must then scatter the animals without raising a great noise. This is a difficult task, made more treacherous by this fat moon. You know, too, that a warrior killed at night dies an unclean death. For this reason, I will order no one to do it."

He stepped up to each of the bucks in turn and they drew their length of reed. When they made their comparisons in the moonlight, they found Touch the Sky had drawn the shortest—and Wolf Who Hunts Smiling the next shortest.

"Perhaps," Black Elk said, "there was medicine behind this decision. Perhaps this is the chance for both of you to show that you think of the tribe first above all else. There can be no fighting now. Do you understand this thing? Your lives depend one upon the other, and Yellow Bear's entire tribe depends on both of you. Do you have ears for my words?"

"Yes, Black Elk," Touch the Sky said.

"I hear you well, Cousin," Wolf Who Hunts Smiling said. But he refused to meet Touch the Sky's eye.

"Go, then," said Black Elk. "You are both on your own. Go on foot and take only your knives. I have been angry with you. But now you go forth to face the glorious death like warriors, like true Cheyenne brothers, and my respect goes with you."

His words swelled Touch the Sky's heart with pride.

Saying nothing to each other, staying well apart, Touch the Sky and Wolf Who Hunts Smiling began following the Powder upriver toward its confluence with the Yellowstone, where the whites had made camp.

The going was easy in the moonlight. The gentle murmur of the current was enough to cover the sounds of their rapid movement. Despite the fear that dried his mouth, Touch the Sky felt himself wondering if this mission would be enough to melt Wolf Who Hunts Smiling's heart toward him, to soften his hard feeling.

But as they rounded the final bend before the camp, he forgot about everything except their incredible luck: the sentry had momentarily abandoned his post to sneak down close to the river for a smoke. This was their chance to kill him without revealing themselves first. Killing at night was not the Cheyenne way. But the goal of this mission was to save the entire tribe from destruction.

"He is mine," Wolf Who Hunts Smiling whispered. "Remember which reed I drew."

Touch the Sky nodded, squatting behind a boulder. Wolf Who Hunts Smiling glided silently forward like a wraith in the moonlight. Touch the Sky heard only a surprised grunt, then saw the glowing tip of the paleface's cigarette drop into the water. Moments later Wolf Who Hunts Smiling returned, his furtive eyes keen with triumph. A bloody scalp dangled from one hand.

"I have made your task easy," Wolf Who Hunts Smiling boasted. "Now I will wait for you here while you complete the mission. But remember that another sentry walks along the far side of the corral toward the mountains."

"You have done well," Touch the Sky praised him. "I will scatter their horses to the four directions of the wind!"

He removed his knife from its sheath and crept silently

forward across the open grass, staying low and relying on hummocks and natural depressions. He could hear the occasional nickering of the horses. Beyond the corral, the camp was covered in a dome of orange light from the many blazing fires. Men laughed and talked loudly in their drunkenness, someone played a harmonica.

Touch the Sky reached the rope corral without incident and started to saw through the strands of hemp. Suddenly he heard a voice in the darkness.

"What in blazes! Who's tossin' them damn rocks? That you, Jake?"

Hurried footsteps thudded closer through the grass. The other sentry was nearing his position! Touch the Sky crouched down as low as he could, his face breaking out in cold sweat. Confused, he turned to glance over his shoulder toward the river. He was just in time to see Wolf Who Hunts Smiling hurl another stone, alerting the sentry.

A moment later the second guard had spotted him in the clear moonlight. In the few seconds it took the white to gather his senses and raise the alarm, Touch the Sky leaped forward and brought him down.

The sentry lost his rifle when he went down. Touch the Sky managed to cover the man's mouth with one hand, stifling his first shout of alarm. But the former mountain man was huge and strong and used to groundfighting. He drew his knees up to Touch the Sky's chest and hurled him free.

"Innuns!" he shouted to the rest of the camp. "Up and on the line! Innuns are in the camp!"

Touch the Sky leaped for him again just as the white drew his Bowie. The well-honed tip sliced Touch the Sky's chest deeply. Anger mixed with desperation drove Touch the Sky's own knife deep into the man's rib cage, and the sentry went slack.

There was no time to take a scalp. Already men were spilling out of the camp circle, their rifles spitting fire. His chest blazing with white-hot pain, Touch the Sky broke for the river. Fortunately he made the cover of the thickets before he was spotted. He was not surprised to note that Wolf Who Hunts Smiling had deserted him.

He swam with the current so the whites could not pick up a blood trail and follow him. The ice-cold river water felt good against this wound and stemmed the bleeding somewhat. But by the time he reached the cold camp, it was clear that Wolf Who Hunts Smiling's lies had done their damage.

"Did you scatter their horses?" Black Elk demanded.

"I could not," Touch the Sky said hotly. "Your cousin deliberately alerted the sentry."

"Alerted him?" Black Elk held up the scalp in the moonlight. "Is this what you call alerting him? Wolf Who Hunts Smiling risked his life to make the mission easier! How can you speak in a wolf bark against him?"

Glancing around at the accusing faces of the others, Touch the Sky realized he was trapped. No one would believe his story. Such treachery as Wolf Who Hunts Smiling had demonstrated could not be believed, particularly when he had lifted the hair of an enemy. So instead he simply stared at Wolf Who Hunts Smiling and directed his words to him.

"Your cousin knows that I do not speak in a wolf bark. This night, again, he tried to kill me. He has shamed me in the eyes of all the rest. The time will come when we fight a fair fight, and at that time I will not merely cut him. I will carve his heart out of his chest!"

Dawn was still a pink blush on the eastern horizon when the persistent hooting of an owl woke Touch the Sky. He sat up, surrounded by the ring of dried brambles he used to protect himself during the night, and listened closely. The hooting grew closer. He rose and stepped out from under the shelter of the limestone outcropping. The others still slept behind him. The air was cool and pimpled the skin around his crudely wrapped knife wound.

He glanced right and saw, through the river mist, a rider approaching. He rushed back under the outcropping and woke Black Elk. As soon as he touched his arm to shake him, the warrior sat up with a knife in his hand.

"Quickly," Touch the Sky whispered. "Someone approaches!"

Black Elk rose from his buffalo robe and grabbed his rifle. Touch the Sky drew his Colt and stepped out behind him. But the owl hoot sounded again, right on them this time, and he realized it was a Cheyenne wordbringer from Yellow Bear's camp. Moments later they recognized Little Shield of the Panther Clan, a youth who had only 11 winters behind him.

"Black Elk!" he greeted the war chief, relief clear in his tone. "For nearly two sleeps I have searched for you. I was told only that I would find you in the Powder River Valley."

"This is a dangerous place to be wandering about, little brother," Black Elk said sternly. "Why have you been sent?"

"You must return to the village at once. We have been attacked by the paleface devils, and several elders and children were killed. And Black Elk—the whites have stolen Honey Eater!"

His words struck both Black Elk and Touch the Sky with the force of a fist. For a moment, their animosity forgotten in the shock of hearing this news, the two Cheyenne exchanged a long, troubled look.

When the others woke, they retrieved their ponies from a hidden copse downriver. Eating pemmican and dried fruit on horseback, stopping only to water and rest their ponies, they made the long ride back to the camp. But Touch the Sky did not once notice the hard journey. He could think only of Honey Eater, wondering if she were even still alive.

They were the last band of warriors to return, and the camp crier announced a council as soon as they had arrived. Exhausted and filthy from the journey, Touch the Sky took his place along the back wall with the rest of the junior warriors.

Old Yellow Bear had clearly suffered greatly since the abduction of Honey Eater. Arrow Keeper and another elder supported him on their shoulders as they entered the council lodge. The lines in the chief's face had deepened, and lack of sleep had left his eyes puffy and redrimmed.

Arrow Keeper greeted Touch the Sky with a nod. Then he conducted the opening ritual in Yellow Bear's place, filling and smoking the pipe before he pushed it toward the headmen. When all had smoked to the four directions, Yellow Bear rose and spoke.

"Brothers! By now all have heard of the misfortune which has befallen our camp. While you warriors were returning, a Lakota word-bringer arrived with a message."

Touch the Sky leaned eagerly forward, torn between anxiety to hear of Honey Eater and fear she was already dead. Black Elk did the same.

"Honey Eater is alive," Yellow Bear said, as if reading their thoughts. "Or so the white devils claim. Their terms are hard. If I call off the war against them, Honey Eater will be returned unharmed. If I do not, she dies a horrible death."

Touch the Sky's immediate relief at hearing Honey Eater

was alive gave way to a sense of hopeless dread. Yellow Bear's horrible dilemma was clear to all. His love for Honey Eater was being pitted against his duty to the tribe. The father in him was at war with the chief. Any attempt to save his daughter might result in the destruction of the tribe. Yet, any effort to save the tribe from the white men's treachery would result in his daughter's death.

A murmur filled the council lodge as the warriors and headmen discussed this. Yellow Bear folded his arms under his blanket until all was quiet again. Clearly, judging from his next remarks, he had given great thought to this matter.

"Brothers, hear me well! Your chief has had his life and feels no fear about leaving this world for the next. I will ride out alone to the whites and offer myself in exchange for Honey Eater. It is the just way. I have served my ten winters as your chief, and as you know, the chief-renewal ceremony will be held with the next melting of the snows."

The headmen and the warriors were stunned. Though Yellow Bear's words showed wisdom, it was essential to the tribe that their chief, like the sacred Medicine Arrows, be protected.

Arrow Keeper rose and spoke. "Brothers, I have heard Yellow Bear's words. He shows both great courage and great love. But does he show great wisdom in this matter? I think the feelings in his breast have ruled his head. This scar-faced white devil will simply kill Yellow Bear *and* Honey Eater. He will collect the bounty on their scalps, then turn to the task of killing the rest of us.

"Brothers! Count upon it, these paleface murderers are wily like the fox. Consider how easily they slipped past our sentries and raided our camp. I, too, love Honey Eater. I love her like my own daughter. If I believed that dealing with the long knives would return her safely to us, I would counsel

113

for this. But these white men do not speak the straight word. I counsel for that which they do not expect: an attack on the camp where they hold Honey Eater prisoner. Thus she may die, but all of my medicine tells me she will die anyway if we trust white men."

Silence fell over the lodge like a shroud. Every man present considered these words carefully. No man in the tribe, not even Yellow Bear, was respected more for his wisdom than Arrow Keeper.

It was Black Elk who next rose to speak. "Fathers! Brothers! Listen to your war chief. I have ears for Arrow Keeper's words. Yellow Bear is a brave man and loves his daughter with a love as deep as the Great Waters. But in his desperation to save her, he has blinded himself to the treachery of the white man."

Black Elk paused before his next remark, his fierce dark eyes fixing on Touch the Sky. "No man here loves Honey Eater better than I. I counsel with Arrow Keeper, and I counsel for war! My band have proven themselves capable braves and warriors. They understand the arts of silent movement and surprise attack. A large war party would announce its presence and be doomed to fail. Our only opportunity lies in a surprise attack on the paleface stronghold. As your war chief, I will lead that attack!"

His words met with great approval from both the warriors and the headmen. Even Yellow Bear nodded his head. The headmen approved Black Elk's plan with a unanimous voice vote.

Now, at least, the tribe had a plan for attempting to save Honey Eater. But Touch the Sky felt no relief as he filed out of the council lodge behind the others. He was exhausted from the recent hard ride, afraid for Honey Eater's safety, and almost completely rejected by the tribe thanks to Wolf Who Hunts Smiling's treachery. With Honey Eater gone and perhaps dead, old Arrow Keeper was his only remaining friend. His fortunes had not sunk this low since the time when he was first captured, tied to a wagon wheel, and tortured over fire.

He stepped outside and found Arrow Keeper waiting for him. The old medicine man touched his shoulder and led him aside. He looked nearly as miserable and dejected as Touch the Sky.

"Come to my tipi," he said, his voice heavy with weariness. "There are important words I must speak to you."

Chapter 12

"You are a brave now," Arrow Keeper said, "a warrior. You have smoked from the common pipe with the headmen. There are certain things you must know now."

With surprising agility in one so old, Arrow Keeper lowered himself until he was sitting with his ankles crossed. He invited Touch the Sky to share the stack of buffalo robes with him. Daylight streamed in through the smoke hole at the top of the tipi and through the tipi cover itself, which was nearly transparent with age.

"I have already mentioned to you," the old shaman said, "the vision which was placed over my eyes at Medicine Lake, the center of the Cheyenne world. Do you recall this thing?"

The troubled young Cheyenne nodded his head. Arrow Keeper's vision told the medicine man that there would never be peace between red men and white men. Great suffering was in store for all Indians. During cold moons yet to come, the Cheyenne would be forced to flee into the frozen lands to the north. The old ones would freeze with the Death Song on their lips.

"When I told you of this vision," Arrow Keeper said, "I spoke also of a great Cheyenne chief named Running Antelope. He and his wife Lotus Petal were killed in a surprise Bluecoat attack. It was reported also that their infant son was killed with them. However, my vision spoke differently. This young man still lives. And the day comes when he will gather the Cheyenne people from all their far-flung hiding places and lead them in one last, great victory for the *Shaiyena* tribe."

"Where is this brave Cheyenne?" Touch the Sky said bitterly, thinking only of Honey Eater and her plight. "We could use him now."

For a moment, Arrow Keeper's sad face almost seemed to break into a smile. "His medicine sign is the ferocious badger," he said. "And we will know him by the mark he carries on his body—an arrowhead. The sign of the warrior."

Touch the Sky started at the reference to the badger. His own medicine pouch contained a set of sharp badger claws, which Arrow Keeper had instructed him to carry. His surprise deepened to curious suspicion when the medicine man rummaged around in a chamois bag and produced a narrow shard of mirror, part of the spoils from a raid on a white man's freight wagon.

He held the mirror just above Touch the Sky's forehead so that the youth had to raise his eyes to see it. Then Arrow Keeper's gnarled fingers gripped his dark bangs and pulled them back sharply, causing Touch the Sky to wince.

"Look closely," Arrow Keeper said.

Now Touch the Sky vaguely remembered, when he was much younger and his white mother used to comb his hair, her remarks about a birthmark on his scalp. It was almost completely hidden by his thick hair. With Arrow Keeper pulling the hair well back and the light from the smoke hole striking it flush, he could clearly make out the mulberry-colored shape.

A perfect arrowhead! The mark of the warrior.

Touch the Sky was struck silent with wonder. Arrow Keeper resumed his explanation.

"I have also already told you that you must face great trials and hardships before your triumph. This, too, was part of the vision. And now I understand that this terrible thing with Honey Eater is one of those trials. But no longer can my vision alone guide you. You must now seek your own medicine vision."

There was no time, the shaman went on, to return to Medicine Lake far to the east. First Touch the Sky must rest along with the others in Black Elk's band. In one-and-a-half sleeps they planned to ride out toward the scar-faced white man's stronghold, which the scouts had located in the Bighorn Mountains just west of the Bighorn river. But before he rode out with them, Touch the Sky must purify himself with a sweat bath. Then, Arrow Keeper instructed him, he must ride to a nearby lake and fortify himself in solitude for the upcoming ordeal.

"I will explain to you what you must do when you reach the lake," said Arrow Keeper, "but be warned: a medicine vision can be either a revelation or a curse. We do not always understand what *Maiyun* tells us to do. His orders might not seem clear at first. Or worse, an enemy's bad medicine may place a false vision over our eyes, and we may act upon it, aiding our enemies and destroying those whom we seek to help."

A light feather of fear tickled Touch the Sky's spine as he thought of something. "Does this mean," he said, "that your vision about me could be a false vision?"

His tanned and wrinkled face troubled, Arrow Keeper nodded. "Medicine visions are powerful things. But sometimes the people's belief in them is abused. Dishonorable Cheyenne have killed red brothers and escaped the tribal law by claiming *Maiyun* told them to do it in a vision. And you must understand that, once you seek a vision and it comes, you must do what *Maiyun* tells you to do. If you do not, and it is a true vision, not only will Honey Eater die, but you shall surely go *Wendigo*. Or if *Maiyun* shows mercy, you will merely die."

Touch the Sky was deeply troubled. "But how can I know if I have experienced a true vision?"

"It is a matter for the heart to decide. But sometimes, if *Maiyun* is benevolent, there will be a sign that the vision is his. Watch for this."

"What kind of sign?" Touch the Sky persisted.

But Arrow Keeper only shook his silver head. "I have exhausted words. You will know if it comes. Now go rest. I will wake you in time for your sweat bath and the journey to the lake."

Reluctantly, the tall youth returned to his own tipi. Despite the worries and fears chasing around inside his head like frenzied rodents, he fell into a deep, dreamless sleep.

It seemed only moments later when Arrow Keeper shook him awake. But the ring of light around the smoke hole of his tipi had turned a deep blue-black with twilight. Arrow Keeper gave him the simple directions for reaching the nearby, isolated lake. He also gave him instructions for obtaining

119

the vision he sought. Touch the Sky was to ride there under the cloak of darkness and remain until first light.

But first he purified himself with a sweat bath in the covered lodge beside the river. The hot steam drained the tension from his muscles and calmed him for the ordeal ahead. He rubbed himself down with sage, rinsed in the cold water of the river, then separated his dun from the pony herd, and rode southwest toward the foothills and the lake Arrow Keeper had spoken of.

When he arrived, the moon was well up, glistening an oily yellow on the placid surface of the lake. It was completely surrounded by oak and cedar trees. Loons raised their eerie cries, and now and then a fish broke surface with a splash that carried easily in the cold, still air.

He tethered the dun with a long strip of rawhide. Then, following Arrow Keeper's instructions, he stripped naked and waded out into the lake.

The air was cold against his naked skin even before he felt the water. But the lake itself felt even colder. His skin quickly went numb as he waded out up to his neck and turned toward the east and the direction of the rising sun.

At first Touch the Sky's mind was filled with thoughts of Honey Eater, of the war party setting out soon, and of the things Arrow Keeper had said. But soon the numbing cold seemed to penetrate his mind, too, taking over all of him. His skin shriveled in protest, his teeth chattered, the cold sliced into him like tiny knife blades.

The moon moved slowly across the burial shroud of the night sky, trailing twinkling stars behind it. Slowly, gradually, the cold numbness became almost a pleasant warmth, and the emptiness inside his mind was replaced by dream images.

He saw the faces of his white mother and father, of the pretty girl he had once loved, Kristen Hanchon. He saw the freckled face of his boyhood friend Corey Robinson, whose madman's antics had frightened the Pawnee attackers and saved Yellow Bear's tribe from destruction. He saw the white-bearded countenance of Old Knobby, the hostler who had prevented a Bluecoat officer from killing him.

These images floated past like wraiths, like ghosts of smoke, and in their place came Honey Eater with her amber skin, beautifully sculpted cheekbones, and luxuriant black hair braided with white columbine.

Following quickly upon this image came the vision that he sought. It came to him in one moment, entire, and then it was gone. One moment his mind was empty; the next he knew everything he was supposed to do. The knowledge shocked him, disturbed him. For the vision told him that he would have to defy Black Elk, defy the tribal law, or Honey Eater was surely doomed.

With this vision came full awareness of his surroundings again. The pleasant warmth of the night was gone, replaced by a bone-numbing cold. His teeth were chattering so hard they sounded like hailstones rattling in the treetops. Startled, he saw that the sky over the eastern horizon was pink with the promise of the new sun.

Stiffly, his muscles protesting in harsh pain, he made his way toward shore. His limbs felt as if they were weighted down with stones. He removed the blanket from his horse and wrapped himself in it, glad for the animal warmth still clinging to it. Then, exhausted, he fell to the ground and slept.

It was an uneasy sleep, filled with troubling thoughts and images. Again and again the vision ran through his head, plaguing him with uncertainty even in sleep.

Had it been a true vision, or the result of his exhaustion, of evil but strong medicine? Arrow Keeper's words returned over and over, a disturbing litany: "Bad medicine may place a false vision over our eyes, and we may act upon it, aiding our enemies and destroying those whom we seek to help."

Suddenly, a loud crack of thunder startled him awake. It was daylight, but the sky had clouded over. Huge black scuds of cloud raced across the sky like a herd of galloping buffalo. The wind had picked up, turning the undersides of the leaves out as it always did before a hard rain.

Touch the Sky knew he should start riding, storm or not. But he was still frozen with tormented indecision. The vision he had received, if accepted, meant defying the highest authority of the tribe. If he rejected such a dreadful course, he might be defying an even higher authority: *Maiyun*. In this case he would be killing Honey Eater, helping to destroy the tribe, and ensuring his own destruction.

Muttering thunder gathered itself into a huge crash that echoed through the foothills. Jagged scepters of white lightning raced across the sky.

Again Arrow Keeper's voice drifted back to him: "Sometimes, if Maiyun is benevolent, there will be a sign that the vision is his. Watch for this."

After another huge explosion of thunder, large raindrops started falling, pimpling the surface of the lake. A sudden, intense flash of lightning made Touch the Sky look straight overhead into the black dome of the storm.

He felt the hair on the back of his neck stiffen when he realized what he was beholding.

For the space of at least five heartbeats, the lightning bolt formed a perfect arrowhead.

Death Chant

* * *

The storm abated by the time Touch the Sky was halfway back to camp. The sun broke through and baked his limbs in welcome warmth. He made it back to the Tongue River village just in the nick of time. Black Elk's band was preparing to ride out.

"The scar-face's camp in the Bighorn Mountains will not be easy to approach," Black Elk was saying as he rode up. "We must cross a vast expanse of short-grass prairie to reach it, exposing ourselves to great danger. Our enemy's sentries may spot us, or scalp-hunters may attack. Each of you must watch the horizon, listen for danger, stay close to the others."

Black Elk directed his fierce attention toward the furtive Wolf Who Hunts Smiling and Touch the Sky. "There will be no fighting among yourselves. Is this thing clear?"

All five in is band nodded. Black Elk took his place at their head and led them west out of the camp. Many in the tribe ran along behind them for a distance, wishing them well. Yellow Bear, framed in the entrance of his tipi, raised his red-streamered war lance high in farewell. Black Elk returned the salute.

When they had forded the river and reached the edge of the wide plains, Black Elk dropped back for a moment. He rode so close to Touch the Sky that the younger Cheyenne could clearly see the crooked stitches where Black Elk had sewn his own detached ear back on with buckskin thread and an awl.

"Hear my words well," the war chief said. His voice was held low so that only Touch the Sky could hear him. "I know full well your feelings for Honey Eater. But I am your war leader. You will forget your love for her and do only as I command. Do you understand?"

Judd Cole

Again, despite the encouragement of the celestial sign, Touch the Sky felt terrible doubts concerning what he was about to do. But the vision was a higher law and must be obeyed at all costs. Even if the lightning sign itself was only part of a false vision, he was determined on his course of action and nothing would sway him.

He averted his eyes now, ashamed of the lie. "I understand," he said, "and I will obey."

Chapter 13

The scar-faced white had instructed Yellow Bear to send the Lakota word-bringer back with word of his decision. A Cheyenne chief could not lie, not even to an enemy. Therefore the word-bringer could not be sent, or his arrival would mean immediate death for Honey Eater.

Instead, the answer would come in the form of Black Elk and his band. They rode hard, due west toward the jagged spires of the Bighorn Mountains. The first day's ride brought them safely across the prairie and into the foothills. The only danger was a squad of Bluecoat pony soldiers patrolling near the Bighorn River. But Black Elk spotted them in time, and his band sheltered in river thickets until the soldiers had passed.

That night they found a cave big enough to shelter them and permit a fire. After a meal of jerked buffalo and ripe chokecherries, each Cheyenne attended to his weapons.

Wolf Who Hunts Smiling had been triumphant ever since the incident with the white sentries. Now that he, too, had a white man's scalp dangling on his breechclout, Swift Canoe was again befriending him. Even Little Horse and High Forehead were occasionally nodding to him. Touch the Sky was the only one who was alone.

His quick, furtive eyes mocking Touch the Sky, Wolf Who Hunts Smiling made a great show of cleaning his rifle—as if to once again remind Touch the Sky that once it had been his.

"I will kill many whites," he boasted as he wiped trail dust out of the breech with a patch of chamois cloth. "One bullet, one enemy. And if I fall, it will be on the bones of a paleface."

More than fear for Honey Eater filled Touch the Sky's breast. There was also the raw bitterness of rejection. It was this empty sense of solitude, of being shut out of the white man's world, that had sent him into the wilderness to find the Cheyenne. Now where would he go? There was no place left for him. An Indian without a tribe was a dead Indian.

And after he had done what his vision told him to do, he would surely be an Indian without a tribe.

However, he reminded himself again that he had no choice. The medicine vision had spoken. He could only pray that it was a true vision and that he might save Honey Eater. If that could be accomplished, then the threat of death held no sting for him.

"Sleep now," Black Elk commanded, "for tomorrow we rise even before the sun. According to the scouts' report, the scar-face's camp lies less than half a sleep away. Because he waits for the word-bringer, we know that he will not slip away to another camp before we arrive. Drink much water tonight."

The Cheyenne were notorious late sleepers; so before important occasions they filled their bladders with water. The need to relieve themselves would wake them early.

By the time the sun was high enough to make shadows the next day, Black Elk's band had entered the Bighorn Mountains. The scouts had left signs for them to follow—notches in the trees or rings where bark had been stripped off. When they stopped at midmorning to water their ponies in a mountain streamlet, Black Elk gathered his warriors around him.

"We are close to our enemy's camp. They are located over the next ridge in the saddle formed between two mountains. Sentries will be posted. From here, remove your bright blankets and never once leave the shelter of the trees. Follow me, and open your eyes and ears to every sight and sound. We must not lose the element of surprise. Nor can we attack until we have studied their camp carefully. Should they once learn of our presence, all hope is lost. We are too few to overwhelm their numbers and weapons."

Touch the Sky's heart sank at these words. If he failed at what he was about to do, he would surely ruin the band's chance to launch a surprise strike.

They resumed their silent trek down the side of the forested mountain. Touch the Sky had been riding last since they set out from Yellow Bear's camp. Now, absorbed in the watch for their enemies, none of the others noticed when he started falling farther and farther behind.

They reached a deep ravine. One by one the Cheyenne angled their ponies around it. High Forehead was riding ahead of Touch the Sky. When he saw High Forehead's pony disappear in the oak trees, Touch the Sky suddenly reined his pony to the left.

The surefooted dun picked her way quickly down the mountain, each step placing more distance between Touch the Sky and the others. Soon he was alone—alone with his misery and his fear and the awful realization that he had just defied Black Elk, his war chief. But in the midst of his misery came the image of Honey Eater.

He chided himself, for his thoughts must be set on nothing else except saving her. He set his mouth in a grim, determined slit and rode in the direction of his enemy's camp.

Touch the Sky moved as quickly as he dared. He knew he must arrive at the camp first and strike before Black Elk could. His medicine vision had already assured him that a strike by the war party would surely kill Honey Eater.

Several times he hobbled the dun and climbed trees to reconnoiter. At first, even after he had cleared the final ridge Black Elk spoke of, there was no sign of a camp. His fear began to grow that Black Elk might track him down before he could strike.

But finally he found the scar-face's camp. And when he did, every hope of rescuing Honey Eater was dashed out of him. The discovery came the fourth time he climbed high up in the branches of an oak tree to scout the terrain. Until then the white men's camp had been sheltered by a thick copse of trees. Now, by chance, Touch the Sky had selected a tree at the perfect angle to glimpse beyond the shelter of trees.

As Black Elk had said, the camp was positioned in the saddle formed by two mountains. The sides were too steep to scale easily, cutting off any attack from the east or west flanks. To the north, behind the camp, aspen and birch trees grew so thick that no mounted assault could possibly succeed. The only approach was from the south. And in that direction the whites had concentrated their defenses.

Imposing breastworks had been erected in a strong perimeter, with at least two well-armed whites behind each set of sharpened logs. The camp was crawling with whites. Each carried a rifle, and most wore a brace of pistols. Their horses and mules were gathered in a rope corral well behind the breastworks.

His heart pounding in his ears, Touch the Sky fought back tears of grief when he failed to spot Honey Eater. Had they already killed her? If so, Touch the Sky vowed that he would at least kill the scar-face before taking his own life.

But suddenly hoped surged in his breast when he spotted her. He had not noticed her, at first, behind the two guards posted to watch her. They had not bothered to tie her up. She sat on a buffalo robe under a golden-leaved aspen tree. It was well behind the breastworks, toward the rear of the camp. Anyone attempting to free her would have to cover the entire camp.

The impossibility of the situation struck Touch the Sky in its full force. Any raid by Black Elk and his band would surely be doomed; the medicine vision had spoken truly on that score. But how could he alone hope to have any better chance?

As he climbed down from the tree, he reminded himself either he placed faith in the medicine vision or he did not. The vision had foretold that if he entered the camp alone he would rescue Honey Eater and they would escape alive. He must dwell only on that thought and nothing else. Otherwise, fear would turn his muscles too weak to be of any use.

By now the sun was westering, growing dim as she sank beneath the spires of the Bighorns. Touch the Sky fortified himself with jerked buffalo from his sash, drank cool water from a nearby stream. As the light began to grow grainy with twilight, he began his final preparations.

He found ripe serviceberries and crushed handfuls of them. He smeared the juice on his skin to cut reflection from the moon. Then he removed the Colt Navy pistol from his legging sash and made sure the firing mechanism was clean and functioning. Finally, he found a flat stone and spat on it. Then he removed his knife and carefully honed the edge until it was lethally sharp.

After that came the awful task of waiting. Darkness had settled completely now, a deep blackness there under the trees where no moonlight broke through. He knew, however, that the camp would be well lit from the full moon and the blazing fires.

When the noises from the camp had finally tapered off, Touch the Sky began his first movements forward. Before he did, however, he gathered his courage by reciting the simple battle song that Walking Coyote had sung upon discovering his brother, Buffalo Hump, dead in the trail:

"Only the rocks lie here and never move.

The human being vapors away."

He moved as silently as he could, protected by the cloak of darkness. But soon the trees began to thin out as he approached the campsite, and silver shafts of moonlight forced him to a low crawl. He edged around a clump of hawthorn and felt his breath catch in his throat. There, outlined in silhouette only three feet away, was a sentry!

Touch the Sky fought down his panic and thought quickly. He could perhaps spend much time backtracking to avoid the man. But if he killed him there would be one less threat should he and Honey Eater choose this route of escape. His mind made up, he slid his knife out of its sheath and coiled his muscles to leap.

He struck straight and true, sliding his blade between the fourth and fifth rib and into the heart as Black Elk had instructed him and the other youths. The sentry gave out only a surprised sigh as his final breath escaped his lips. He slumped dead, blood spuming from his chest.

As badly as he wanted the firepower, Touch the Sky decided to leave the sentry's long Henry rifle behind. There was no way he could easily carry it and still move silently along the ground. Besides, any fighting he did that night would be close in, where a pistol would be best. Unfortunately, the sentry wore no short iron.

Heartened by this kill, he continued forward. It took a long, agonizing time to reach sight of the breastworks. Now he was completely in the open moonlight. Fires blazed in the camp, throwing eerie, long shadows from the pointed tips of the breastworks.

He saw that he could not hope to penetrate the fortifications directly. This meant slipping around at either end. Yet, again, a sentry waited at each point.

The lefthand side was more in darkness; so he chose that route. His heart racing in fear at the dreaded exposure, he crawled inch by slow inch across the clearing. At every moment he expected a warning shout and the blazing of many rifles.

Finally, mercifully, Touch the Sky had crawled to within yards of the sentry. The white man sat on a tree stump, his rifle propped between his knees. He was playing a jew's harp, holding it in his teeth while he plucked it.

Touch the Sky gathered himself to leap. Suddenly, a stick underneath his elbow snapped loudly. The guard dropped his jew's harp and strained his eyes into the darkness in front of him. Touch the Sky was still on the ground when he realized he had been spotted.

He leaped at the same moment the sentry raised a shout of alarm. Touch the Sky rammed his head into the white's ample gut, knocking the wind out of him before he could finish his shout. But in the confusion when they toppled, Touch the Sky ended up on the bottom with his knife hand pinned under him.

Their flailing legs had already kicked the sentry's rifle off into the surrounding brush. Once, twice, a third time the strong white man brought his knee up hard into Touch the Sky's ribs and stomach, battering him painfully. But the determined Cheyenne refused to relinquish his one-handed grip on the man's throat, knowing he was doomed if his enemy shouted the alarm.

He had lost his knife somewhere in the carpet of leaves and debris. But now his right hand was free, and he added it to the death grip on the sentry's throat. Again a knee struck him hard, this time knocking the wind out of him. But like a tenacious wolverine, he refused to loosen his grip on the white man's throat. It seemed to take forever, but finally the sentry lay still beneath him, all the fight gone out of him along with his final breath.

For a long time Touch the Sky lay beside his fallen enemy, gasping and heaving. He feared that the struggling man had injured him too seriously to continue. Pain sank deep knife points into him each time he breathed in or tried to move. Finally, however, the pain abated enough to allow slow and gradual movements.

He was past the breastworks. But the real task lay ahead. He had to cover almost the entire expanse of the camp to reach Honey Eater's robe. Fortunately, most of the men had rolled into their own robes and were snoring in sleep.

But surely someone would soon discover one of the dead sentries? And even if that didn't happen, how would he get Honey Eater back out alive?

"Trust in the medicine vision," he reminded himself fiercely as he recovered his knife and inched past one of the dying fires. Nonetheless, Arrow Keeper's words plagued him over and over: "Bad medicine may place a false vision over our eyes, and we may act upon it, aiding our enemies and destroying those whom we seek to help."

The torturously slow, low-crawling journey seemed to go on forever. Insects bit at his exposed skin; every sound made his heart leap into his throat. But finally, miraculously, he recognized the aspen under which Honey Eater had been sitting. And there, an indistinct shape in the darkness, lay Honey Eater asleep on her buffalo robe.

For the first time, despite the sentries flanking her, hope surged within the youth's breast. Perhaps the vision had spoken truly after all!

Sudden footsteps only a few feet to his right made him press himself flat into the ground.

"I'm going out to check on the guards," a man said.

Cautiously, Touch the Sky lifted his face. In the flickering light of a nearby fire, he recognized the speaker's raw, red, ugly scar. A moment later he was gone, heading out toward the perimeter.

Touch the Sky fought back his welling panic. He could only pray that the scar-faced leader would begin his check with the sentries Touch the Sky had not killed. But even so, he must move fast.

Before he could think what to do, however, two more white men edged into the circle of firelight. Instantly he recognized the two men who had gotten him drunk at the trading post.

"Why don't you two boys go take a long piss?" said the one with the coarse-grained face. "Me 'n' Stone got us a little piece of business with this Injun filly. We won't be long."

One of the sentries offered halfhearted objections until coarse-face handed him a small buckskin pouch. "That-air's pure gold dust, hoss. You two split it up even while you're out there takin' a piss. Doan worry 'bout this Injun sayin' nothin' to Lagace. She doan savvy no English."

A moment later the two sentries had slipped off into the shadows beyond the firelight. By now all the talk had woken Honey Eater. Touch the Sky, a cold knot of hate and fear forming in his belly, watched her sit up and draw back against the aspen as she recognized the two new arrivals.

"I paid," coarse-face said to his partner as he began to unfasten his buckskin trousers. "So I'll go first."

Chapter 14

It was all happening too fast for Touch the Sky to form a plan. His eyes flicked from Longstreet to Honey Eater, his mind in a welter of confusion.

McMasters laughed. "You best be quick, Jed. I aim to plant my carrot in her, too, afore Lagace gets back. He figgers to save her all for hisself."

Honey Eater had drawn as close to the tree as she could. From habit, her hand groped for the knife she usually wore around her neck. But Lagace had already removed it. Now, as she turned her face into a stray shaft of moonlight, Touch the Sky spotted the dark, swollen place over her temple where she had been pistol-whipped during her capture.

Longstreet, his aroused breathing whistling in his nostrils, reached out to hitch her dress up. The next moment his head exploded in a burst of bright orange light. He fell at Honey Eater's feet, dead before he hit the ground.

Touch the Sky knew full well that the proud Honey Eater would choose suicide at the first opportunity if she were defiled by these white dogs. He also knew he could not be sure of killing both men with just his knife. A bullet from his Navy Colt had just shattered Longstreet's skull.

The cylinder had revolved to a new shell, but there was no time to insert a primer cap. He dropped the pistol and, knife in hand, leaped on the surprised McMasters.

The huge man was quick for his size. Touch the Sky drove his right arm up toward his vitals, knife in hand. But McMasters caught his arm in a grip as strong as a beartrap. Even through the desperation of his struggle, Touch the Sky could hear confused shouts of alarm all around him. His shot had aroused the entire camp.

Remembering a trick Black Elk had taught his band, Touch the Sky swept his right leg in a hooking motion, his foot catching McMaster's left leg and toppling him. As the big-white man fell, he pulled the Cheyenne down with him.

McMasters yowled in pain as he fell on the edge of the knife blade, slicing his meaty shoulder to the bone. This loosened his grip on Touch the Sky. Now the desperate youth raised his knife for the final, lethal plunge into his enemy.

"Touch the Sky!" Honey Eater screamed. "Watch out!"

But her warning was too late. Lagace brought the butt of his rifle down hard on the Cheyenne's skull; splitting his scalp open and knocking him out cold.

Honey Eater leaped to Touch the Sky's side. Lagace did nothing to stop her. By now a circle of well-armed men had formed around the aspen, craning their necks to see what was happening. Longstreet lay dead, and McMasters was bleeding furiously from his wounded shoulder.

"Don't stand their with your thumbs up your sitters!" Lagace shouted to his men. "Can't you see that Indians have infiltrated our camp? At least three men are dead. You, Beckmann, and you, Rogers—form the men into a skirmish line quick! Hell only knows how many more are out there."

"Well, it won't take long to find out," McMasters said grimly, busy wrapping a strip of deerhide over his wound to stem the bleeding. He had just caught sight of the young Cheyenne's face in the moonlight. "That-air's the buck from the trading post. The one I told you about what speaks good English. We'll by God make him talk!"

Slowly, his thoughts swirling on a river of pain, Touch the Sky opened his eyes. It took him a long time to realize that the glittering white pinpoints overhead were stars blazing in the night sky. His head throbbed hard, the pain like a heavy, sharp weight pressing into the side of his skull. He tried to move his arms and legs, but they were stretched rigid and refused to respond.

For a moment fear lanced through him. Was this immobility death? Had he crossed to the Land of Ghosts? Or, since he had perhaps died without singing the death song, was he trapped forever in the Forest of Tears?

Suddenly, pain exploded in his right ribcage and he tensed. A moment later he realized he was still in the land of the living.

"You cut the wrong hoss, Injun," McMasters said, kicking him again with the toe of his boot. "By beaver, I'm gonna have your topknot danglin' off my sash. But first, you're gonna watch while I leave my jizzom in that squaw of yourn!"

Touch the Sky realized he was staked out spread-eagle beside a roaring fire. He could feel the heat close to his face. His scalp was tacky with half-dried blood from the wound Lagace had inflicted.

The scar-faced leader squatted down beside Touch the Sky. His scar was ugly and raw and jagged in the flickering firelight. "Where's the rest of your band?" he said in English. His voice was surprisingly calm and quiet.

Touch the Sky held his face expressionless and said nothing.

"I know you savvy English," Lagace said. "I said where's the rest of your band?"

Touch the Sky held his silence.

"How many of you are there?"

Still Touch the Sky said nothing. Slowly, casually, Lagace removed the knife from the sheath on his sash. "Is this Yellow Bear's response to my deal?"

Touch the Sky refused to show the fear he felt inside when he saw Lagace stick the blade of the knife into the flames.

"You might just as well talk now, boy. You sure's hell will later," Lagace said.

"That's for damn sure," McMasters said. "You'll talk, Injun. Oh, you'll sing us a tune when we cut your peeder off and feed it to you."

Touch the Sky was aware of other faces watching him, but he could not lift his head enough to see if Honey Eater was all right. Fear had dried his mouth and iced his blood. But he remembered the Indian way, all the times Wolf Who Hunts Smiling and the others had called him Woman Face. Now he refused to let these white dogs see his fear.

"You cooperate with me," Lagace said, still heating the blade in the fire, "you tell me bow many came with you and where they're hiding, and I'll let you go. I'll let you and the girl go."

Touch the Sky knew Lagace was lying. Even if he weren't, the warrior in him would not agree to those terms—not even to save Honey Eater. How could she marry a brave who had forsaken his band?

Lagace finally removed the blade. The very edges were glowing a bright red. He spat on the hot metal, and the liquid instantly sizzled into vapor.

"One last time, buck. Where's the rest of your band, and how many are you?"

Touch the Sky held his mouth in a straight, determined slit and maintained his silence. He tried not to flinch when he felt the heat of the blade approaching his bare chest.

A moment later, his scream rent the dark fabric of the night. The pain was incredible. His body tensed against the ropes like a bowstring drawn tight. There was the crackling sound of cooking meat, the putrid stink of human flesh burning.

McMasters laughed, enjoying this spectacle immensely after the deep gash he had suffered. Finally, mercifully, Lagace removed the burning blade and said, "Tell me, how many did your chief send to kill me?"

Vaguely, even through his pain, Touch the Sky was aware of a woman crying somewhere behind him.

"Honey Eater!" he called out to her in Cheyenne. "Do you know that I love you? Do you know that I have placed a stone in front of my tipi? When that stone melts, so too will my love for you! These white dogs can kill me now, but they will never kill my love for you! I am sorry I did not save you, but be strong. The others may save you yet!"

His head exploded in pain when McMasters fetched him a vicious kick.

"You talk English, Injun, and you talk to us. Doan be hollerin' nothin' out to your squaw or to the rest of the bucks. Can't nobody save your bacon now."

"Shut up," Lagace told his lackey quietly. "I'll handle this. You and Longstreet didn't do such a good job of handling him when you had the chance, did you? Maybe if I untied him right now, you wouldn't be talking the he-bear talk."

Lagace bent closer over Touch the Sky's face. Somehow, in the flickering firelight, his scarred visage made Touch the Sky recall the tales of the devil that he used to hear in the white man's church. Despite his quiet voice and calm manner, this man, the Cheyenne realized, was more dangerous than McMasters with all his blustering talk.

"That knife blade was just a touch," Lagace said. "Just a touch. Either you talk now, or you're going to be in a world of hurt. You won't die fast, buck. I won't let you. You'll go out slow and painful. And before you die, you'll see the girl die too."

Touch the Sky was not sure that the scar-faced devil would kill Honey Eater just yet—not when she was good for bargaining power with Yellow Bear and the tribe. Clearly this white man did fear the Cheyenne. Even now his eyes kept nervously flicking to the surrounding darkness.

But Touch the Sky had no doubt he meant every word concerning him. Still, he held his face expressionless and refused to speak.

Now, for the first time, a note of impatience crept into Lagace's tone. "Put some rocks in the fire," he ordered McMasters. "Heat them until they glow red."

McMasters laughed again and scrambled to carry out the order. Behind him, Touch the Sky could still hear Honey Eater weeping for him. But he knew it was not wise to speak to her again. He only wished she did not have to hear his screams, which were almost as torturous for her as the pain was for him.

Lagace grabbed his head and turned it toward the fire so Touch the Sky could see. He was forced to watch as McMasters, using a stick, rolled several fist-sized rocks out from the coals. They glowed like giant chunks of punk being fanned in a breeze.

"They stay hot for a long time," Lagace said. "We're piling them on you, one at a time, until you tell us what we want to know."

But Touch the Sky no longer cared. He had made his mind up, and nothing would change it. The pain had finally driven him to a point where he was numb to fear.

McMasters, using two sticks now, picked up one of the rocks. A moment later, despite his numbness and determination, Touch the Sky felt pain so intense he could not have believed it possible. It was as if every nerve in his body had been stripped raw and held into a flame.

Again his scream echoed through the night

Black Elk felt conflicting emotions warring inside him. From his position high in an oak tree, he watched the scene below in the paleface camp. The rest of his band were spread out an either side of him, likewise occupying spots high in the trees. They had spent hours crawling down the side of one of the mountains that flanked the saddle in which the camp was pitched. The trees grew thick here, at an odd slant, and the side of the mountain was too steep to easily scale. The only way they could be attacked was from above.

Black Elk had seethed with anger ever since Touch the Sky gave the rest of the band the slip. To violate direct orders from a war chief was serious enough. Cheyenne had been banished from the tribe for this. But now Touch the Sky had ruined any chance for a successful raid on the camp. It was essential to maintain the element of surprise against such overwhelming numbers and firepower. Now that was out of the question. The scar-face would surely know that no Indians—certainly not Cheyennes—would raid alone.

But along with his anger he felt a grudging sense of admiration for the young Cheyenne's skill and courage. Had the brazen young buck not slipped past a formidable line of sentries? Had he not fought against the huge, hairy-faced white man with the courage of a she-grizzly protecting her cubs? And look now how he refused to answer the white dogs' questions in the face of torture terrible enough to kill a lesser brave.

This was the Cheyenne way! Black Elk, too, had been watching Honey Eater when the two paleface devils had made as if to violate her. Despite his reluctance to reveal the position of his band, he had been about to discharge his rifle to stop them. That was when Touch the Sky leaped up from the ground and revealed his presence to Black Elk for the first time.

And when Touch the Sky swore his love for Honey Eater even in the midst of his pain—truly the words had stung Black Elk with jealousy. But was it not a manly vow, expressed from the depths of a good and strong love? They were the same words Black Elk himself might have used. Despite his regret, however, the truth of his earlier vow to Touch the Sky had not changed. One of them would have to die to decide who married Honey Eater.

Even so, Black Elk was a war chief and bound to a high code of honor. His admiration for this upstart, but brave, Cheyenne youth would not let him wish this kind of death on Touch the Sky. And surely he would die at the hands of these white dogs unless Black Elk came up with a plan.

But what? His band was forced to take to the trees like frightened birds. Attacking the camp was impossible. They had been forced to tether their horses a great distance away to avoid detection.

Angered by Touch the Sky's desertion, he had issued strict orders to the rest of his band to stay put. What other choice did they have? Either he came up with a battle plan soon, or Honey Eater, and perhaps all of them, were as doomed as Touch the Sky.

Another earsplitting scream rose as the hairy murderer dropped a second glowing rock on Touch the Sky's chest. Still the Cheyenne refused to talk. Suddenly, Black Elk decided he had seen enough. It would be risky, but he had to earn a rest for Touch the Sky.

He knew that sound carried in odd ways in the night. Turning his head to disguise the direction of his voice, he shouted, *"Hiya, hi-i-i-ya!"*

From the trees surrounding him, the other four Cheyennes in his band dutifully repeated the tribe's war cry: *"Hiya, hi-i-i-ya!"*

A satisfied smile momentarily parted Black Elk's normally stoic face as he watched the white scar-face and his henchman leap for the shadows beyond the campfire. Shouts of alarm spread throughout the camp as the palefaces prepared for a charge.

However, Black Elk's elation quickly passed. He had purchased a short respite for Touch the Sky. But now the white dogs knew they were close to their camp. And Honey Eater was no closer to safety.

Soon, Black Elk thought glumly, their enemies might have many more Cheyenne scalps to trade for gold.

Chapter 15

Little Horse had never hated whites more than he hated them now. He had watched through the night, fury boiling inside of him, as the paleface devils had hideously tortured Touch the Sky. Mercifully for the young Cheyenne prisoner, the band's war cries during the night had forced the frightened whites to take a break in their cruel sport.

Clinging in the branches of an oak tree as dawn broke over the camp, Little Horse realized the terrible injustice he had done to Touch the Sky. Had he not accused him of being a white man's dog? Had he not turned his heart to stone against the best friend he had in Yellow Bear's tribe, calling him a traitor to the Cheyenne? And all because the wily white men had tricked Touch the Sky into drinking their strong water.

But watching his friend's strength and courage throughout the horrible ordeal of the night had convinced Little Horse that Touch the Sky was a true and brave Cheyenne brother. He had put his life on the line for Honey Eater, and he had chosen pain worse than death rather than cooperate with his white captors.

Little Horse realized that no matter what it cost, even if it meant losing his own life or honor among the tribe, he must try to help his friend. Little Horse knew he could not live as an honorable brave if he did not try. Nor could he stand the thought of Touch the Sky's dying without knowing that he had a blood brother in Little Horse.

His mind was made up. He would defy Black Elk's order to remain where he was. Little Horse knew that the normally hot-tempered Black Elk, always one for action rather than patience, was reluctant to attack so long as Honey Eater was still alive.

In the gathering light, Little Horse glanced to his left toward the tree where High Forehead was hidden. Two large branches of their respective trees almost touched. Moving slowly, cautiously, Little Horse began shinnying along his branch until he could swing into High Forehead's tree. Little Horse was small for his age, but compact and sure in his movements. He gained High Forehead's position with hardly a rattling of the oak leaves.

"Brother," he greeted him in a whisper so that Black Elk would not know he had left his position, "how do you feel about what you have seen this night?"

High Forehead was also clearly moved. "I feel that we have wronged a brave and true Cheyenne brother," replied the newest member of Black Elk's band. "I will never forget such courage! I am sorry now that I let Wolf Who Hunts Smiling fool me into believing that Touch the Sky is not a true warrior. I am sorry that I did not treat Touch the Sky with the respect he deserves."

"Are you sorry enough," Little Horse said, watching him closely, "to help him?"

High Forehead looked startled. "How? Speak of this."

"I cannot simply let my brother die. I plan to sneak back to where we have left our ponies. I have a plan. But it requires at least two. Will you go with me?"

High Forehead was deeply troubled. He glanced farther down the line toward the tree where Black Elk was hidden. The huge forehead that had earned him his name wrinkled with indecision.

"It means defying our war chief," he said finally.

Little Horse nodded. "It does. But Black Elk is now like a cat with his back arched. He spits and shows his claws and makes a war face. But his concern for Honey Eater's safety prevents him from striking. Meantime, Touch the Sky lies close to death."

"We may be banished from Yellow Bear's tribe."

Again Little Horse nodded. "We may. But brother, I will speak the straight word to you. It is more likely we will die in our attempt. But we will die the glorious death of which Black Elk constantly speaks! As for myself, I would rather die alongside my brother Touch the Sky than go on living, knowing how I wronged him and let him die. You have not forsaken him as I did, and thus you do not owe him as much as I. I understand if you do not wish to join me."

"If I refuse," High Forehead said, "are you going by yourself?"

Little Horse nodded.

"Then the decision has been made for me. It has been cruel enough watching the paleface dogs torture Touch the Sky. I will not remain up in this tree like a frightened squirrel and watch you die, too."

Death Chant

High Forehead's words filled Little Horse with pride for the courageous young Cheyenne. "We have no rifles, only our bows and lances," said Little Horse. "But I swear by all the power of my medicine bundle that we shall smear our bodies with white man's blood! Come! But move quietly. If Black Elk spots us he may stop us."

Moving cautiously, the two Cheyenne descended from the tree. The trek ahead of them was long and arduous. First they had to scale the long, steep slope of the mountainside. Then it was a long journey to the place where they had tethered their ponies. It might well be too late by the time they made it back—Touch the Sky and Honey Eater could very likely be dead by then.

And even if they did make it back in time, Little Horse knew his plan was far more desperate and courageous than practical. It was like two skinny coyotes attacking a den of grizzly bears.

The sun was blazing overhead by the time they made it up the side of the mountain. They had covered half the distance to the copse where their ponies were hidden when suddenly a horse nickered and sent them leaping for cover.

Then Little Horse realized that he recognized the whinnying. It was Touch the Sky's dun! He investigated behind a thick deadfall and found the pony. This was a stroke of good fortune. As he untethered the pony, High Forehead said, "What is this?"

Little Horse glanced at the medicine bundle tied to the dun's hair bridle, the polished antelope horn hanging around its neck. He could also still see, faintly, the outlines of the magical symbols Arrow Keeper had drawn on the pony's flanks with charcoal.

For a moment hope surged in his breast. Little Horse suspected that *Maiyun* had intended for them to find Touch

147

the Sky's pony. "It is strong medicine," he said. "I believ
that Arrow Keeper has given this pony magical powers
Have courage, brother. We may not be riding into battl
alone."

Lagace was filled with a murderous fury.

He knew he and his men were surrounded by Cheyenne
but how many? And where exactly were they? He had bee
on edge ever since their war cries had sounded during th
night. Now it was midmorning and still there was no sig
of them.

He glanced across the central camp clearing at the sti
form of the Cheyenne buck they had taken prisoner. Seein
him, Lagace's face seemed to take on some of the livi
coloring of his scar. When the youth had finally passe
out from the pain, Lagace realized he was not going t
talk. The youth's chest and stomach were covered wit
raw, blistering burns, but still he had not given in.

His men were jittery and nerve-frazzled from the ordea
of waiting. This worried Lagace. These were not discipline
soldiers loyal to a cause. They were cutthroat mercenarie
following another cutthroat mercenary. Their only loyal
ty was to themselves and his pocketbook. And all thi
trouble with the Cheyenne had forced him to curtail hi
whiskey-peddling and scalping-for-bounty activities. Gol
was scarce, and the men were starting to grumble.

A shout came from the perimeter sentries. "Ride
approaching!"

Lagace tensed, drawing his Colt-Patterson pistol. But
moment later the sentry's voice added, "It's Jennings, fro
the Yellowstone camp!"

A tall, lanky rider with a full red beard guided his piebal
around the breastworks and into the middle of camp. "W

got Injun troubles," he said to Lagace as he dismounted. "McPherson sent me to tell you. I'da been here sooner, but I run into Sioux bands twice and had to backtrack to save my topknot."

"Hold on," Lagace said. "You have any trouble riding into camp just now? See signs of any redskins close by?"

"Here? Naw . . . I'm talkin' 'bout trouble up to the Yellowstone camp."

Lagece frowned. If they were surrounded, why would Cheyenne let a paleface break their ranks? But it might be a ruse. Maybe they wanted him to do what he was tempted to do: divide his numbers and send men out to scout. Then the Indians would attack a weakened camp.

"What kind of trouble?" he said finally.

Jennings stared at the unconscious Cheyenne. "Trouble like that right there. We got a band of Cheyenne warriors picking us off. They've killed five men so far, and we ain't been able to draw a drop of their blood."

"How many are there?"

Jennings shrugged. "I'll be earmarked and hog-tied if I can tell! Seems like them red sumbitches is everywhere, but you never see 'em. The men are gittin' spooked. A bunch of 'em are ready to rabbit plumb out of Injun country. Can't make no money when you're busy hunkerin' down."

Lagace frowned again, but said nothing. He glanced back over his shoulder and made sure the guards were keeping a good eye on the Cheyenne girl. He was beginning to understand that he had made a mistake in abducting her. Those Cheyenne hidden outside of camp had not come to parley.

On the other hand, if there were enough to attack, why hadn't they done so? It was about time to bring things to a head. He was already losing control of the men at the other camps, and soon there'd be a mutiny here. It was time to fight it out with the hidden war party, then take the fight right to Yellow Bear's camp.

"Go tell the cook to feed you," he told Jennings, dismissing him. He called Stone McMasters over from a group of men gathered behind the breastworks. "You still got that Sioux arrow you been hauling around?"

"Damn straight," McMasters said. "That's my lucky arrow. Went plumb through my hat 'n' parted my dander for me."

He lifted his floppy plainsman's hat to show the white crease on his pate. Lagace ignored it. "Bring me the arrow," he said.

He called one of the guards over and instructed him to bring the girl over to where the Cheyenne prisoner was tied spread-eagle. Then he walked over to the unconscious Indian and emptied a canteen of water in his face.

Touch the Sky started awake, then immediately winced at the fiery pain wracking the middle of his body. The scar-face named Lagace was staring down at him, his face grim with determination. A moment later Touch the Sky's eyes widened, for Honey Eater was standing beside him, each arm pinned by a white sentry.

McMasters joined the group and handed the arrow to Lagace. It was fletched with white feathers, the shaft painted blue in honor of the Sioux's sacred lake in the *Pahasapa* or Black Hills. The tip was a wide, sharp piece of flint.

"All you men!" Lagace shouted to the camp at large. "Keep your eyes skinned good now! Might be an attack coming!"

He turned to Touch the Sky again. "You're a strong Indian," Lagace said. "Got a real set of oysters on you, just like the Cheyenne buck that opened my face up. Now we're going to see just how tough you really are."

He seized Honey Eater from the sentries and held her by a handful of her thick black hair. With his other hand he removed his knife from the sheath at his waist. He ordered McMasters to cover Touch the Sky with his rifle while one of the guards untied the prisoner's bonds.

"All right, then," Lagace said. "Let's see what kind of leather you got in you. Apache warriors kill themselves by ramming an arrow down their own throat. Let's see if you're as tough as an Apache. I'm giving you a choice. Either you shove that arrow down your gullet, or I scalp the girl right here in front of you."

Chapter 16

Despite the horrible pain wracking his body, Touch the Sky felt even worse in his heart. His eyes drank in what was probably his last view of Honey Eater. Though she did not speak one word of English, she clearly understood the dilemma they were in. She realized that Touch the Sky was about to die and that she would probably die soon after. She tried to be brave like him. But tears streamed from her eyes.

Touch the Sky knew it was useless to pretend he didn't understand what Lagace had said to him. The white men knew full well that he spoke English. Besides, something was dangerously different in Lagace's manner. He was not bluffing. If Touch the Sky tried to play the fox, the white devil would scalp Honey Eater before his eyes.

"Last night," Honey Eater said, her eyes filled with pity as she looked at his horrible burns, "even in the midst of your pain, you swore your love to me. And do you know that I love you, brave Cheyenne warrior? There is room in my heart for no one but you. If you must die, then I will die too. We will meet in the Land of Ghosts, where no white men can separate us."

She crossed her wrists over her breast—Indian sign talk for love.

"I must die," Touch the Sky conceded. "But you must not give up on life just yet. Even now Black Elk is watching you. It is only fear for your safety which has kept him from acting. But he will act when he sees that your death is at hand. And when he does, you must be prepared to seize the moment. It is your only chance."

"Quit the palavering," Lagace said. "I've given you your choice, buck. Now make it, and make it quick. Elsewise, I'll make it for you."

He tightened his grip on Honey Eater's long hair to make his point. She winced at the pain. Touch the Sky had to force himself not to leap at the scar-faced dog. This was no time to force Lagace's hand. He needed to buy all the time that he could in hopes that Black Elk and the others were even at this moment moving into position or formulating a desperate plan.

"Eat that arrow, Injun" McMasters said, grinning so wide that his broken yellow teeth showed through his beard. "If you can't get it all the way down, I'll shove it the rest of the way for you."

Touch the Sky gripped the shaft in both hands. He was on his knees now, the rest facing him. He stared for a moment at the flint arrowhead, noticing how wide, yet sharp, it was. The thought of ramming it into his throat made an involuntary spasm start in his stomach. He looked away.

"Make up your mind," Lagace said. He expected any attack to come from the only approach, in the direction of the breastworks. So he held Honey Eater in front of him as a human shield against bullets.

"Gonna taste damn good," McMasters said. "Even better 'n that whiskey we poured into you at the tradin' post." He laughed and added, "You wait too long, red Arab, and you're gonna see a white man ruttin' on your squaw."

Despite this taunting, Touch the Sky held his face emotionless in the Indian way under pressure. Bravery now was important, not only for his own pride as a warrior, but as an example to Honey Eater.

"Last time I'm telling you," Lagace said. "Make your choice, or I raise the girl's hair."

Tears were streaming from Honey Eater's eyes, and she could not control the sobs that shook her body. Touch the Sky knew this was the moment of his death. He also knew that he would not pray to the white man's God, but die an Indian.

He gripped the arrow even tighter and began reciting the Cheyenne Death Chant.

> "Nothing lives long
> Only the earth and the mountains."

Even as he sang the sad words, a voice at the back of his mind told Touch the Sky the bitter truth: his medicine vision at the lake had been a false vision after all, evil medicine placed over his eyes by his enemy.

For a moment one hand left the shaft of the arrow and moved down to touch his medicine bundle for the last time.

When he heard Touch the Sky singing the death song, Black Elk's face twisted in an agony of indecision. His rifle was aimed at Lagace. At the first sign that the white dog was going to harm Honey Eater, he would kill him.

But he must wait. So long as Honey Eater had breath in her, he could not risk her life. Though his anger at Touch the Sky was immense, here was yet one more sign of his bravery. Black Elk understood the choice Touch the Sky had been given and recognized the horrible death he had bravely chosen to inflict upon himself.

Black Elk would cut off his own hand if he could do something to save Touch the Sky! The war chief was a man of action, not accustomed to this infernal sitting and waiting and watching. And no doubt action would come soon enough. As soon as Honey Eater was clearly in danger of immediate harm, he and Wolf Who Hunts Smiling, the only ones with rifles, would fire on the camp. Then all five Cheyenne would leap from their trees and charge down onto the whites, even if it meant all of them would die.

Black Elk imitated the owl hoot to warn the others to prepare themselves. Immediately, Wolf Who Hunts Smiling and Swift Canoe responded. Black Elk frowned when Little Horse and High Forehead failed to hoot back from the last two trees. He repeated the sound, a bit louder. Still no response came.

What did this mean? Had they shown the white feather and sneaked off to safety? Black Elk doubted this cowardice, especially of Little Horse. The small Cheyenne was large in courage and one of Black Elk's favorites in the tribe. And High Forehead, though still unskilled in some things, was brave beyond his years.

But surely they too had not willfully disobeyed their war chief's orders as Touch the Sky had done? Even amidst all the danger he faced, the certain hopelessness ahead, Black

Elk felt wrath burning inside him. If, by some miracle of *Maiyun,* they survived this ordeal, those who had disobeyed Black Elk would face serious consequences.

This thought, however, was brief and fleeting. Black Elk concentrated on the scene below. He held his rifle sights trained an Lagace's chest, exposed at this angle despite his cowardly use of Honey Eater as his shield.

Touch the Sky threw his head back and raised the arrow over his face. Never had he needed courage as he did at this moment. His arms trembled in rebellion at the thought of doing this thing to himself.

He took one final breath to fortify himself.

Now.

"Hiya, hi-i-i-ya!"

Shouting their fierce battle cry, Little Horse and High Forehead burst on horseback from the surrounding trees and bore straight down on the fortified breastworks. Little Horse led Touch the Sky's dun pony by a strip of rawhide tied to its hackamore.

The whites were momentarily caught off guard. They had all turned from their posts to watch the young Indian swallow the arrow. By the time they raised their weapons and started firing, the intruders were almost on them.

Lagace had leaped for cover at the first cry, deserting Honey Eater in his panic. At this point no one could gauge the size of the attacking party.

The redheaded messenger named Jennings raised his rifle to draw a bead on Little Horse. There was a muzzle flash from Black Elk's tree, and the back of Jennings' skull exploded.

"They're attackin' from two directions!" somebody shouted. "They got us surrounded!"

156

Touch the Sky scrambled to his feet, his burned flesh screaming in pain, and ran to Honey Eater's side. Before they could run for cover, the Cheyenne battle cry sounded again. They both looked toward the breastworks just in time to see the strong Indian ponies clear them in magnificent leaps!

But now Little Horse and High Forehead rode into a hail of bullets. Touch the Sky saw Little Horse wince and tilt to one side as a lead ball caught him in the calf. The next volley of fire dropped High Forehead from his pony like a dead weight, blood spuming from a fatal hit in the middle of his chest.

Now Black Elk and the others were charging the camp from the west flank, down the steep, forested slope. They added their war cries to the clamor and confusion, rifles spitting fire.

"They got us boxed in!" someone else shouted. His words triggered panic among the men along the perimeter. Some scrambled on foot into the trees, others raced toward the rope corral for their horses.

"Stand and hold, you white-livered bastards!" Lagace screamed. "We got the numbers on 'em!" But his orders went unheeded.

Little Horse rapidly closed the gap between himself and Touch the Sky and Honey Eater. Expertly, he gripped his pony around the neck with one arm and his one good leg. Touch the Sky watched him slide low on the pony's flank and knew what he had in mind.

"Be ready to ride!" he said to Honey Eater. He gripped her around the waist with one muscular arm and lifted her as easily as if she were a delicate reed.

Barely slowing, Little Horse swooped down and grabbed the maiden when Touch the Sky handed her up behind him. He turned his pony toward the breastworks again. Suddenly Lagace fired his pistol at Little Horse, but his shot went wide.

Little Horse had turned Touch the Sky's dun loose. He had also thrown his battle lance point first into the dirt before he raced out of camp again, spiriting Honey Eater to safety. Touch the Sky tugged the lance out of the ground and called to the dun. Obediently, she raced to his side.

By now Black Elk and the others had created the illusion of a large attack. Most of the whites had deserted the camp. But as Touch the Sky raced toward the breastworks, Stone McMasters stepped out from behind a tree and aimed his long Henry at him.

Touch the Sky was weak and wracked with pain. But Little Horse's courage and skill and High Forehead's sacrifice filled Touch the Sky with the spirit of the warrior. He raised his right arm high, cocking it to unleash the stone-tipped lance.

His aim was true. The lance punched into McMaster's barrel chest so hard that it drove the tip out through his back. The big man stood for a long moment with a surprised look on his face, blood spurting across his lips. When he fell, he landed on the lance and hung in the air at a crazy angle like a half-felled tree.

Despite his desperate desire to get clear of the pit of white devils, Touch the Sky knew he could not leave High Forehead's body among his enemies. High Forehead's pony had already bolted in panic. Touch the Sky pulled his dun up and leaped to the ground, lifting High Forehead and throwing him across the pony's rump.

He looked back once to make sure that Black Elk and the other Cheyenne were escaping too. All of them had grabbed horses from the rope corral. There was almost no fire now from the scattered defenders, and the Indians were racing toward the breastworks shouting their triumphant battle cries.

But Black Elk was searching the entire camp for the same person Touch the Sky wanted to sight: the scar-faced leader named Lagace who had caused all of this death and suffering.

And now Touch the Sky did spot him, only he was already clear of the camp. In the first confusion of battle he had untethered his magnificent sorrel gelding, the animal that he boasted had never lost a race. Touch the Sky paid close attention to the direction in which he was fleeing, marking the course in his mind.

"Fly like the wind!" Black Elk shouted at him as he raced by on his stolen horse. "When the others realize how few we are, they will look for us with blood in their eyes!"

Touch the Sky swung up onto his pony, his burned chest aching like a thousand knife points stuck into him. Then, one hand securing his dead red brother behind him, he fell in behind Black Elk and Wolf Who Hunts Smiling and raced into the safety of the trees. But he was careful to remember the route Lagace had taken. And he vowed that one more white dog would die before his sister the sun had set in the west.

Chapter 17

Black Elk's band rode swiftly down out of the Bighorn Mountains, stopping only long enough to bind Little Horse's wound with strips of soft tree bark.

Pain throbbed in Touch the Sky's burns with each step the dun took. When they finally reached the safety of the foothills, Black Elk ordered a brief halt. They cut two long trailing poles and made a netting of vines and rawhide strips, fashioning a travois on which to haul High Forehead's body.

Black Elk had stolen an extra horse for Honey Eater. She was near exhaustion from the ordeal of her captivity, still in shock from the battle and Touch the Sky's near death. She had ridden in silence, only occasionally glancing toward Touch the Sky as if to reassure herself that he had survived.

Black Elk surprised Touch the Sky by disappearing for a

brief time, then returning with a handful of yarrow leaves. "Pound these into a paste with water," he said, handing them to Touch the Sky, "and rub it on your burns."

He turned away before Touch the Sky could thank him. The young Cheyenne found two heavy rocks and did as he was instructed. Almost immediately the cool paste soothed his burns.

The band reached the broad open flats of the plains just as the sun melted into a glowing red blush on the western horizon. There was no sign they were being followed. By now Honey Eater was falling asleep on horseback, so Black Elk ordered them to make a cold camp for the night.

"I killed one enemy for every bullet I fired," Wolf Who Hunts Smiling boasted after they had all rolled into their robes for the night. "And if the paleface dogs had not scattered like frightened crows, I would have killed more with my knife."

"And I sent two whites under with my arrows," Swift Canoe said.

"You fought well," Black Elk's voice said in the darkness under a sky spangled with glowing stars. "And you obeyed the orders your war chief gave you."

This was his first reference to Touch the Sky and Little Horse's disobedience. Touch the Sky longed to explain that he had not willfully disobeyed—that he had instead followed a medicine vision. But he remembered Arrow Keeper's warning that some Indians used visions as an excuse to avoid punishment for wrongdoing. He remained silent.

"Those who did disobey," Black Elk said, still avoiding names, "fought bravely. Honey Eater has been saved, thanks in part to their courage. But what of the scar-face?

Is he not free to continue his treachery against the red man?"

Touch the Sky knew that his enemy Wolf Who Hunts Smiling was gloating at these words. And Black Elk was right—part of their mission had been to kill Lagace.

Touch the Sky had determined to do just that. He was already in serious trouble for disobeying Black Elk. It hardly mattered if he did it once more. He must kill Lagace. Not only was his hatred for the paleface devil intense, but his medicine vision had told him he alone must kill the scar-faced leader. And now Touch the Sky understood that it was indeed a true vision, a higher power that must be obeyed. Those who sought visions but did not fulfill their commands, Arrow Keeper had warned him, were doomed to death or insanity.

Touch the Sky had lost his weapons in the white camp. But he had already removed from its sheath High Forehead's, a small but sharp obsidian blade attached to a wooden handle. He could feel its weight in his legging sash.

Touch the Sky drank much water that night so that his aching bladder would wake him well before the others. In the soft half-light of dawn he paused for a long moment beside Honey Eater's robe, watching her in sleep. The delicate sculpting of her high cheekbones and her full, heart-shaped lips filled him with love.

Finally, reluctant yet determined, he walked down to the buffalo wallow where they had tethered their horses. The dun greeted him with an affectionate nicker, nuzzling his shoulder with her nose. Despite the soothing yarrow paste his burns were still stiff. He almost groaned out loud as he swung up onto his pony and headed north out of camp.

Touch the Sky was almost certain that Lagace had hightailed it toward the camp at the confluence of the

Yellowstone and the Powder. Since water was scarce hereabouts, he would almost surely follow the Little Bighorn River northeast to the Yellowstone, then turn east and follow the Yellowstone straight to the camp.

By the time the sun was high enough to warm the air, Touch the Sky knew he had guessed correctly. Near the Little Bighorn he had picked up a fresh set of tracks made by an iron-shod horse. Now time was the critical element because Lagace had a swift horse and a good lead. Could Touch the Sky close that lead before the white dog reached the safety of his camp?

He reached down and touched the antelope horn Arrow Keeper had hung around the pony's neck. The medicine man's words drifted back to him now from the hinterlands of memory: "I have just blessed your pony with long wind, speed, and strength."

Touch the Sky dug his moccasined heels into the dun's flanks and urged her to a gallop with a shrill war cry. Within moments he knew the old shaman had spoken the straight word. The dun did not gallop. She flew. Touch the Sky's black locks streamed straight out behind him, the wind whistled past with a sound like a fierce windstorm so powerful it brought tears to his eyes. The ground raced past him, an indistinct blur.

His pony seemed tireless. Her pace did not once abate, and no slope or cutbank was steep enough to lather her. By the time the sun was straight overhead, Touch the Sky spotted a lone rider dead ahead, a mere speck on the horizon.

The distance between them closed rapidly, and soon Touch the Sky recognized the magnificent sorrel gelding. Not until the youth was close enough to also recognize Lagace's long yellow hair did the white man realize he was being followed.

Viciously, he dug his long-rowelled spurs into the gelding's flanks, drawing blood. The sorrel lunged forward from an easy lope to a full gallop.

Still Touch the Sky's dun closed the gap. As the white man turned to gauge the distance between them, the contempt on his face turned to disbelief. His horse was fresh, and he had paced him easily for the journey. Never had he been caught in a race.

When Touch the Sky had closed the gap to perhaps three lengths, Lagace drew his Colt-Patterson and fired. The bullet whizzed past Touch the Sky's left ear with a sound like an angry hornet. The pace was too fast for Lagace to load another primer cap on horseback. Desperately, he dug his rowels into the gelding's flanks.

Lagace swerved toward the rim of a steep cutbank overlooking the river. Touch the Sky nudged the dun over too, now almost close enough to touch the sorrel's sweaty rump. Lagace drew his Bowie just as Touch the Sky drew up alongside him.

Pulling High Forehead's obsidian knife from his legging sash, Touch the Sky made a daring sideways leap off his pony. A moment later he and Lagace hit the ground together and rolled so hard and fast that Touch the Sky felt the wind being knocked out of him.

But he never once let go of his quarry. The white man was incredibly strong and quickly got one big hand on Touch the Sky's throat. His knee raked Touch the Sky's burn-scarred chest, causing a pain as intense as the hot rocks themselves had. The day started going dim as Lagace continued to throttle him.

In one last desperate struggle for life, the Cheyenne youth arched his strong back hard. The quick movement threw Lagace clear. Not wasting a moment, Touch the

Sky leaped on him again and drove the obsidian blade into his enemy's ribs. It slipped smoothly between the fourth and fifth ribs and straight into Lagace's heart. Touch the Sky felt the satisfying release of body heat as he cut into the vitals.

But they had landed on the very verge of the cutbank. As Touch the Sky finally sat up after regaining his breath, the soft dirt bank beneath Lagace gave way. The body dropped straight down into the river and was washed away with the current, streaming ribbons of blood behind it.

There was no easy way down, and Touch the Sky was too exhausted to chase after it. Now he had no scalp to take back and hang on the village lodge pole. But his enemy was dead!

When his muscles finally quit trembling, he set out to round up his pony and the magnificent sorrel. Now, he told himself, with this horse and the gray he had stolen from the Crows, he had the beginnings of a fine bride-price to someday offer Honey Eater.

But first, he reminded himself with a heavy heart, he must face the consequences of his disobedience.

By the time his shadow was long in the waning sun, he was heading east toward the Tongue River and Yellow Bear's camp.

"Brothers!" Chief Yellow Bear said. "The charges against these two young Cheyenne are grave. You have heard Black Elk describe what they have done. You have seen also that neither of them accuses Black Elk of speaking with a double tongue. Now have ears for my words."

Seven sleeps had passed since Touch the Sky's return to camp. Now the councillors and warriors were formally meeting in their lodge to discuss the fate of Touch the

Sky and Little Horse. The two young Cheyenne had been instructed to sit in the center where all could stare at them. The common pipe had been smoked, and the sweet, fragrant smell of burning willow bark hung over the lodge.

"Brothers!" Yellow Bear said. "Lakota word-bringers have arrived with joyous news. The white men have removed their talking paper which offers gold for Cheyenne scalps. There is no sign of this scar-face or his dogs who sell strong water to the red men. Touch the Sky claims to have killed him, and I have never known this young buck to speak in a wolf bark.

"All of these things are important to the tribe. And now an old man would add this: Honey Eater has been returned safely to her people. It is a serious thing to disobey a war chief, a terribly serious thing. But it is even more serious to banish a Cheyenne from his people. Consider these matters carefully before you vote with your stones. Now I have spoken, and you have kindly listened."

The lodge was silent until Wolf Who Hunts Smiling rose to speak. "Fathers! Brothers! I am young, and my words carry small weight. But this troubles me. No one here has seen Touch the Sky kill this scar-faced dog! Where are his weapons, his scalp? True, Touch the Sky returned with a horse, but who among us has not stolen a horse from our enemies?"

A few of the councillors nodded at this, and Wolf Who Hunts Smiling said, "Not only did he disobey the orders of a warrior, but of a war chief! And now High Forehead wanders alone in the Forest of Tears, killed before he could sing the death song. He lost his life because Touch the Sky and Little Horse willfully disobeyed their leader!"

This time a low murmur filled the lodge. Chief Yellow

Bear folded his arms until it was quiet again. Old Arrow Keeper, seated to the left of Yellow Bear, looked troubled but said nothing.

Touch the Sky felt the old hatred for Wolf Who Hunts Smiling boiling inside of him. But he forced himself to hold his face impassive and say nothing. As Arrow Keeper had already advised him before the council met, he must place his trust in Arrow Keeper's vision at Medicine Lake. His fate was already determined, and his actions would not affect it.

Now Black Elk rose. "Fathers! Brothers! Place my words in your sashes and take them away with you. I have told you what these two young braves have done to disgrace the Cheyenne way. But I have also told you that their courage and skill in battle have made my heart sing. I, for one, do not doubt Touch the Sky when he claims to have killed the scar-face. I ask only this. When you vote with your stones, do not judge them for their lack of manly courage. Ask yourselves only this: have their crimes been sufficient to send them forever away from the tribe? Remember, too, that High Forehead will never smoke the common pipe with us nor bounce his child upon his knee. I have spoken."

His last words filled Touch the Sky with an agony of remorse. He would never forget that magnificent moment when High Forehead leaped the breastworks, bravely shouting the war cry. Nor the awful moment when he had died.

Yellow Bear rose for the final time. His voice weary, he said, "Enough! Let the headmen speak with their stones."

Arrow Keeper moved among the 20 voting headmen offering them a fur pouch. It contained 40 small stones. Each councillor reached in and selected the stone of his choice: a white moonstone to signify forgiveness, a black agate if he chose banishment. He kept his choice hidden in his closed hand. When all had chosen, Arrow Keeper handed the half-empty pouch to Chief Yellow Bear. The chief spilled the contents out onto the buffalo robe at his feet.

Twenty stones rolled out: ten white and ten black.

The lodge broke into a clamor until Yellow Bear again crossed his arms. "Brothers! In such cases it is usual for your chief to cast the final vote. But you all know well that Honey Eater is the soul of my medicine bag and thus my vote would not be a fair one. Clearly I do not desire to banish these young men. However, many will resent them—and me—if I use my authority in this way. Instead, let their war chief cast the deciding word."

The lodge grew so silent Touch the Sky could hear his heart thumping in his ears. He glanced at Little Horse and saw his friend's lips trembling with the effort to disguise his emotions. Black Elk was a fair leader, but a hard one. His sense of honor and duty caused him to make his heart like a stone toward his emotions.

A Cheyenne without a tribe, Arrow Keeper had said, was a dead Cheyenne. Now, with the choice of a moment, Black Elk would determine if they lived or died.

Arrow Keeper crossed to Black Elk and offered the pouch. Black Elk hesitated for a long moment, his fierce black eyes trained on Touch the Sky. "Now," Touch the Sky thought bitterly, "comes his chance to win Honey Eater from me forever."

Black Elk reached in, made his choice, and tossed the stone onto the robe with the others. Every neck craned to see. Suddenly the lodge buzzed with excited talk.

Yellow Bear crossed his arms until all were silent. "The voting is done, and now the tribe has spoken with one voice. From this time forward, all discussion of this matter is over."

He picked up the white moonstone Black Elk had chosen. "Little Horse and Touch the Sky are *Shaiyena* warriors and members of Yellow Bear's tribe. The stones have spoken!"

Still, Touch the Sky held his face impassive. But inside, a great weight had been lifted. His eyes met Little Horse's, and for a brief moment a smile touched his friend's lips.

But Black Elk was not smiling when he took Touch the Sky aside as he exited the lodge. "I had no choice but to vote as I did. In banishing you, I would also have banished Little Horse, whom I admire greatly. All assembled today know full well that we both love Honey Eater. Had I voted as my heart told me to, it would have appeared that I used my power to steal her from your arms. Know this, you are a brave and strong warrior, but in my mind you are still far from acceptance as a good Cheyenne!"

Black Elk turned away and left him. His words quelled the elation Touch the Sky had felt inside the lodge. So did the realization that Wolf Who Hunts Smiling had seethed with bitter anger when Black Elk chose the white stone. He had vowed to kill him, and Touch the Sky knew they would soon have to confront each other for good.

"There will be many trials and many sufferings," Arrow Keeper had told him. Would he never gain acceptance? His heart heavy with sadness, he returned to his tipi.

He lifted the elkskin flap over the entrance, and his gloomy face broke into a smile.

There, just inside the entrance, sat a horn cup filled with wild bee honey. Fresh white columbine petals had been arranged in a perfect circle around the cup. He felt his heart surge with renewed hope.

Honey Eater loved him, and he had a home. He was a Cheyenne, and though his future was still uncertain, he was no longer an outcast among the whites. He had chosen to make his stand here, among his own people.

Let the trials and sufferings come. With Honey Eater's love to guide him, he was ready.

WILDERNESS

GIANT SPECIAL EDITION:
HAWKEN FURY
by David Thompson

Tough mountain men, proud Indians, and an America that was wild and free! It's twice the authentic frontier action and adventure during America's Black Powder Days!

AMERICA 1836

Although it took immense courage for frontiersmen like Nathaniel King to venture into the vast territories west of the Mississippi River, the freedom those bold adventures won in the unexplored region was worth the struggle.

THE HOME OF THE BRAVE

But when an old sweetheart from the East came searching for him, King learned that sometimes the deadliest foe could appear to be a trusted friend. And if he wasn't careful, the life he had worked so hard to build might be stolen from him and traded away for a few pieces of gold.

__3291-0 $4.50 US/$5.50 CAN

DOUBLE WESTERNS
A Double Blast of
Rip-roarin' Western Action!

TWO CLASSIC TALES OF ACTION
AND ADVENTURE
IN THE OLD WEST
FOR THE PRICE OF ONE.
One Heck of a Value!

TRAIL TO HIGH PINE/WEST OF THE BARBWIRE
By Lee Floren.
__3183-3 $4.50

CHEYENNE GAUNTLET/INDIAN TERRITORY
By David Everitt.
__3194-9 $4.50

GUNSHOT TRAIL/TEXAS TORNADO
By Nelson Nye.
__3234-1 $4.50

BROOMTAIL BASIN/TRAIL TO GUNSMOKE
By Lee Floren.
__3262-7 $4.50

LEISURE BOOKS
ATTN: Order Department
276 5th Avenue, New York, NY 10001

Please add $1.50 for shipping and handling for the first book and $.35 for each book thereafter. N.Y.S. and N.Y.C. residents, please add appropriate sales tax. No cash, stamps, or C.O.D.s. All orders shipped within 6 weeks via postal service book rate. Canadian orders require $2.00 extra postage. It must also be paid in U.S. dollars through a U.S. banking facility.

Name _____
Address _____
City _____ State _____ Zip _____
I have enclosed $_____ in payment for the checked book(s).
Payment <u>must</u> accompany all orders. ☐ Please send a free catalog.